Trevor he

Following the sound, he twisted the knob on the basement door and used his keys to unlock it. He jerked the door open.

Steff rushed straight into his arms and remained there for several seconds before shoving him away.

"That wasn't funny," she declared.

"What are you talking about? How did you get stuck in there?"

"You were snooping and locked me in."

"I was not snooping. And I did not lock you in. That's the truth."

Suspecting him was natural, Trevor supposed, since no one else was supposed to be here at this time of night.

"But...if it wasn't you, then who was it?"

* * *

REUNION REVELATIONS: Secrets surface when old friends—and foes—get together.

Books by Valerie Hansen

Love Inspired Suspense

Love Inspired

VALERIE HANSEN

was thirty when she awoke to the presence of the Lord in her life and turned to Jesus. In the years that followed she worked with young children, both in church and secular environments. She also raised a family of her own and played foster mother to a wide assortment of furred and feathered critters.

Married to her high school sweetheart since age seventeen, she now lives in an old farmhouse she and her husband renovated with their own hands. She loves to hike the wooded hills behind the house and reflect on the marvelous turn her life has taken. Not only is she privileged to reside among the loving, accepting folks in the breathtakingly beautiful Ozark mountains of Arkansas, she also gets to share her personal faith by telling the stories of her heart for Steeple Hill.

Life doesn't get much better than that!

Hidden In
The Wall

VALERIE HANSEN

Steeple
Hill®

Published by Steeple Hill Books™

Special thanks and acknowledgment are given to
Valerie Hansen for her contribution to the
REUNION REVELATIONS miniseries.

STEEPLE HILL BOOKS

Steeple
Hill®

ISBN-13: 978-0-373-44274-4
ISBN-10: 0-373-44274-2

HIDDEN IN THE WALL

A friend loves at all times,
and a brother is born for adversity.
—*Proverbs* 17:17

This book *has* to be dedicated to the five other
marvelous authors who participated in this series:
Shirlee McCoy, Margaret Daley, Carol Steward,
Lenora Worth and Marta Perry!

PROLOGUE

A friend loves at all times, and a brother is born for adversity.

—*Proverbs* 17:17

Trevor Whittaker swung the boom of the backhoe and took more and more bites of earth. If he hadn't been paying such close attention, he might have missed feeling a momentary stutter of the equipment. Concerned, he peered at the partially dug trench then climbed down to take a closer look.

Steff had left a spade leaning against the building, so he grabbed it instead of returning to his truck for his own tools. The blade had connected with something hard. It looked like…

Trevor's breath caught. He dropped the shovel and fell to his knees, frantically clawing at the earth. With trembling fingers he brushed aside enough dirt to be certain his imagination wasn't playing tricks on him.

He reeled back on his haunches, appalled. These weren't water or electric lines he had unearthed, they were bones. Human bones!

Suddenly a shadow fell across the trench. Trevor leaped to his feet, blocked Steff's view with his body and grasped her arms to control her. "Don't look."

She tried to twist free. "Why not? Let me go."

"No. There's…" He thought about trying to distract her instead of revealing his gruesome find, then realized she'd never accept anything but the truth. "There's a skeleton in the trench," he said hoarsely. "It's a grave."

ONE

Two months prior

Slightly lifting the skirt of her pale blue satin gown so the hem wouldn't brush against the asphalt, Stephanie Kessler picked up her evening bag, left her car in the parking lot of the Mossy Oak Inn and started toward the inn's ballroom. This was not just another of the many gatherings she organized for Magnolia College as the Alumni Relations Director. It was also the ten-year reunion of her own graduating class and she wanted everything to be perfect.

Steff paused long enough to check her slim, jeweled watch. She'd been so eager to renew acquaintances she'd arrived far too early. Rather than waste time pacing inside the inn or rearranging the lovely table decorations for the umpteenth time, she decided to stroll across to her office on the opposite side of the campus.

Not only was the balmy June evening ideal for a leisurely walk, she reasoned, the exercise would help her unwind. And checking her e-mail would show her whether she'd had any last-minute answers to her recent pleas for alumni financial support. In spite of recent fund-raisers, she was still coming up short on donations for the planned library expansion. That was worrisome.

A welcome breeze lifted Steff's short blond hair away from her cheeks. When she faced into the wind to take advantage of its refreshing coolness, her gaze rested on the imposing stone edifices of the college that had become the central focus of her life.

Campus was nearly deserted this time of year, which was why she was surprised to notice a tuxedo-clad figure whom she didn't recognize hurrying around the far end of the liberal arts building.

Assuming from his attire that he must be planning to attend the gala at the inn, she noted he was headed in the wrong direction.

Since she had plenty of time to spare, Steff decided to do her good deed for the day, follow him, and help him find his way to the reunion.

The height of her heels and the unevenness of

the old brick walkway slowed her progress. By the time she got to the next corner her quarry was already disappearing past the science building.

The newer walkway in that area was a flat cement surface and she was able to travel faster. She proceeded as far as the quad and paused, puzzled. Shading her eyes against the setting sun, she squinted as she studied her immediate sur-roundings. The man couldn't have vanished into thin air. So where had he gone? Could he have ducked into one of the buildings they'd passed? Since no classes were in session this time of year, that didn't make sense. Besides, why on earth would he want to hide?

Feeling foolish for having followed a stranger halfway across campus, she decided to give up and resume her trip to her office. That was when she spotted him. He'd been temporarily out of sight because he'd been bending over next to the east wall of the library and the foundation plant-ings had masked his position.

The man was pacing now, as if measuring the distance from the library wall to the sidewalk. What in the world could he be up to? Stephanie asked herself. More importantly, who was he?

The setting sun backlit his form, making him

appear in silhouette and causing her eyes to water when she tried to stare directly at him. The one thing she could tell was how furtive his movements were. Whatever he was doing, he obviously didn't want to be observed.

Internal warnings sounded in her brain and caused her to shrink into the shadows. Whoever he was, it would definitely be best if he didn't know she'd been spying on him.

Steff's nose tickled. *Stupid allergies.* She pressed her index finger across her upper lip to keep from sneezing. Her quarry had returned to the sidewalk and seemed to be walking along it with measured strides. Then he wheeled and repeated his path to the library wall at a right angle before he turned again.

Although she believed she was well hidden around the corner of the building, she held her breath. The man had stopped and seemed to be staring directly at her. Was he? Had he sensed that she'd been trailing him? She didn't see how he could know she was here, yet his stillness and apparent concentration gave her chills.

When he finally moved away from the library wall, she relaxed slightly. Now he was wiping the soles of his shoes on the lawn. That particular planted area was in deep shade, perfect for azaleas but often overly wet, especially after the kind of spring rains they'd had the past few days. He'd probably gotten his shoes muddy.

Steff shifted her own feet slightly, thankful she'd had the good sense to remain on the grass.

The unmistakable sound of masculine cursing drifted to her across the distance. She stiffened. She was about to backtrack to avoid encountering such an ill-mannered man when her nose took control. A violent sneeze erupted before she could stifle it, so powerful it bent her over at the waist.

She straightened. Froze. Gaped and stared across the intervening space at the man she'd been studying. He, too, had ceased all movement. Then he took a step toward her and began to peer into the shadows where she hid.

For a heart-stopping instant Steff thought he might actually be planning to launch an attack. She held her breath and stood stock-still, hoping she wouldn't sneeze again just in case he hadn't really spotted her. Her palms were damp, her pulse fluttering, her muscles tensing for flight.

A split second later she knew the tuxedo-clad man had other plans. He whirled suddenly and ran, disappearing quickly around the corner of the library.

Still frightened in spite of the logical conclusion

that he didn't want a confrontation any more than she did, Steff turned and hurried in the opposite direction, back toward the inn.

The shadows created by the Spanish moss hanging from the trees reached out for her like clawing fingers of gray smoke. Every tree seemed to hide an unnamed menace, every footstep seemed to echo as if someone—or something—was closing in behind her.

She grabbed a handful of skirt to raise it out of her way enough to run, not caring that her high-heeled shoes were not designed for sprinting.

Every instinct insisted she had to get away. It didn't help that she saw no one in pursuit when she glanced over her shoulder. The danger was there just the same. She could feel it all the way to her bones.

"We have a problem," the caller said.

"I can't see how."

"Well, I can. I just paced it off. Unless they decide against building that annex by the east wall, the way they've planned, the new construction is liable to reveal everything."

"Then see to it that they change their minds."

"How can I do that?"

"I don't know and I don't care. Just do it. Use your

influence as much as you have to. We both know we can't allow them to do a lot of digging there."

"It might be okay if they don't go too deep or too far past the corner. I can't remember exactly where the other trench was, can you?"

"Yes. But I'm not about to show up on campus and take the chance of ruining everything. You're there. You handle it."

He cursed as he stared at the phone in his hand. This was ridiculous. It shouldn't be his problem. He'd briefly considered using violence to keep their secret but he knew there was no guarantee that either of them would get away with another so-called accident. They'd been pressing their luck so far. It was bound to run out eventually.

"All right," he finally said. "I'll try."

"I suggest you do more than merely try. I suggest you succeed. Or else."

"Or else what?"

"You don't want to find out."

As he hung up he grimaced, then mustered his self-control, turned and headed for the gathering at the inn.

Steff had touched up her makeup and managed to compose herself outwardly by the time the reunion guests began arriving. She hoped that her carefully poised demeanor was adequately masking the tremors that continued to shoot through her every time she recalled her scare by the library. She didn't want anything to mar the festivities she'd worked so hard to plan, especially not her overzealous imagination.

Steff stationed herself by the main entrance to personally welcome new arrivals and was pleased to recognize old friends. "Cassie! Kate! How wonderful to see you both again! It seems like forever." She gave each of them a big smile and a sisterly hug. "I'm so glad you could make it."

"We wouldn't have missed this reunion for anything," Cassie said. She eyed Steff. "Great dress. Of course, if I had your millions, I could look like that, too." She giggled. "Not."

"I assure you, I don't have control of the Kessler checkbook," Steff countered. "If I did, I'd probably just pay for the library addition instead of arranging all those fund-raisers."

"I see your point," Kate chimed in. She took Steff's arm and drew her aside. "Who else do you expect tonight?"

"Quite a few of our old friends, like Jennifer

Pappas and Dee and her sister Lauren. Unfortunately, I wasn't able to locate everyone from our class."

Cassie waggled her eyebrows. "How about the guys? I suppose Mason and Parker are too rich or too famous, or both, to show up."

"Actually," Steff said, "I know Parker is planning to come. Have you driven by the Magnolia Hall mansion and seen the way he's restored the grounds? I can only imagine what the inside looks like. I hear it's awesome."

"It would be nice to see Parker again," Kate said wistfully. "I always thought he was…interesting."

"Speaking of interesting," Cassie drawled, aiming a grin at Steff. "Have you seen your former roommate, Alicia, lately? I hear she and her big brother Trevor are both back in Magnolia Falls."

Blushing, Steff nodded. "As a matter of fact, I've not only seen her, I've asked Whittaker Construction for a bid on some remodeling I'd like done in my office."

"Aha!" Cassie was clearly enjoying the moment. "I knew it. You always did have a thing for Trevor Whittaker, even if he was forever getting into trouble."

"I mentioned the job to him for Alicia's sake,"

Steff insisted. "He's supporting her while she goes back to school and gets her teaching credentials."

"Trevor is? Why?" Cassie asked.

"Because Alicia's husband left her high and dry four years ago when her boys were just babies."

"And you're only hiring Trevor for Alicia's sake? Is that what you're trying to make us believe?"

"It's true!"

Both Kate and Cassie chuckled softly.

Thinking of Trevor raised fresh goose bumps on Steff's arms. Admittedly, there was something about that man that set her on edge. Though she had done her best to deny it, there had always been a kind of peculiar mutual fascination between them.

Beginning to smile at the ridiculousness of her thoughts, Steff rejected them outright. She was a mature woman of thirty-two, not a naive girl. If Trevor Whittaker thought he could still rattle her these days, he'd better think again.

"Uh-oh," Cassie drawled. "Speaking of good-looking men."

Steff's head snapped around. Her eyes widened. Alicia had apparently chosen her big brother as her escort because she and Trevor were coming through the double doors together. His dark hair was slicked back, yet still retained its wavy charm, and the tuxedo he was wearing set off his broad shoulders in a way Steff couldn't help but admire. The man was more than impressive-looking tonight. He was breathtaking.

Smiling broadly, she greeted Alicia as she surreptitiously eyed the one man who could make her knees weak with a mere glance. Thankfully, she'd always been able to mask her feelings and appear unaffected by him, and tonight was no exception.

She kissed Alicia lightly on the cheek, then smiled at Trevor. "Welcome to our reunion. I imagine you know most of the people here." She gestured toward her nearby friends. "Remember Cassie and Kate?"

"Of course. Good evening, ladies." Trevor's attention returned to Steff. "And good evening to you, Ms. Kessler."

His unusually formal demeanor caught her off guard so she reverted to well-practiced dialogue. "Please, go on in and make yourselves at home. There's lemonade and a buffet of delicious appetizers. We'll be serving our main course later."

As Trevor took his sister's elbow and escorted her into the ballroom, Steff eyed him appreciatively, until her gaze drifted to his shoes. There was a smudge of mud on one of the heels. Georgia clay and loam. Just like the dirt in the flower beds next to the library.

Stunned, Steff felt her balance waver for a split second. Her friends immediately crowded closer.

"What's wrong?" Cassie asked. "You look pale."

"Trevor's shoes," Steff said in a stage whisper. "Look. There's mud on them."

"I'm not a bit surprised," her friend answered. "After the storms we had the last few days the whole campus is pretty soggy." She pointed. "See? Half the men in the room have traces of mud on their shoes, even some of our illustrious professors."

Although Cassie's assessment was clearly correct, it did nothing to calm Steff's jangled nerves. Surely, Trevor wouldn't have run from her, she reasoned, yet if it wasn't him messing around by the library, then who was it? And why had the shadowy figure frightened her so?

She huffed in self-disgust. From the looks of it, the nameless trespasser could be almost any man in the room.

That realization brought another shiver and a feeling of unidentifiable dread she couldn't seem to dispel. An evening that should have been filled with joy and celebration was turning out to be a lot more disconcerting than she'd imagined.

Shivering, Steff wrapped her arms around herself. The most sensible thing to do would be to simply ask Trevor how he'd gotten his shoes dirty.

Yes, she countered, *but what if it was him by the library? What then? Would I have to ask him what he was up to? Suppose I didn't like his answer?*

Entertaining the mere *notion* that Trevor had been skulking around campus was unacceptable. Not knowing, one way or the other, seemed infinitely better than having to face the unpleasant possibility that he might have been the one who had frightened her out of her wits.

TWO

Trevor arrived on campus the following Monday, as planned. He was far from overjoyed, however, at the prospect of having to return to Magnolia College for even a short period of time.

He certainly didn't have many pleasant memories of his younger days here, nor did he view the place with the affection and reverence Steff always had. The university had her family's influence stamped all over it. Some of the massive live oaks even bore plaques giving credit for their planting to a long-dead Kessler.

He muttered under his breath as he parked and climbed out of his truck, then was immediately penitent. "Sorry, Father," he prayed quietly as he walked toward the offices. "I know I should be thankful for every job You give me and I did ask for more work, it's just that I hadn't counted on having it be *here*."

The one aspect of Magnolia College that he did miss was the Campus Christian Fellowship. Some of the friends he had made while attending those CCF meetings were still close and many had gone on to join the nearby Magnolia Christian Church where he also worshipped.

Finding faith on the road to maturity had given Trevor a purpose and had helped straighten him out. How anybody managed to cope day-to-day, let alone face trauma, without an abiding belief in God amazed him. Personally, he didn't know what he'd do if he didn't have his strong beliefs to fall back on when the going got tough.

And speaking of tough going, he mused, it was time to enter the lion's den. Squaring his shoulders, he pushed open the main door to the Administration building, strode in and proceeded directly to Alumni Relations.

Stephanie was seated behind a desk piled high with stacks of paper and files when he knocked and entered.

She stood and extended her hand in greeting. "You're prompt. I like that."

Trevor considered making a wisecrack, then

stifled the urge. This was business, not playtime in the quad. "I take my work seriously."

He shook her hand as briefly as he dared. He didn't want to offend her, but he also didn't want to be tempted to stand here holding her hand and gazing into her beautiful, violet-blue eyes like a lovesick teenager. It was bad enough that she was wearing a pale silk blouse that enhanced those eyes and tailored slacks that looked as if they'd been made just for her—which they probably had, he added, disgusted with himself for noticing.

"So, show me the wall you want remodeled," he said, taking a pencil and pad from his shirt pocket and unclipping a tape measure from the waist of his jeans.

"Sure. Over here." Steff pointed. "See all the wasted space? I thought, if there was a bookcase recessed into the wall behind the door, I could take advantage of every inch of this cramped little office."

"You probably grew up with clothes closets that were bigger," he said wryly.

"As a matter of fact, I did." She watched him measuring and making notes. "What do you think? Can it be done?"

"Anything can be done," Trevor said. "It's a question of how difficult or expensive it may be. I can have an estimate for you in a few minutes. There's no obligation. If you decide you want the work done, I can start right away. If you put it off and call me later, I'll do my best to squeeze you in, but I can't guarantee when."

"Fair enough. How long to you think the whole job will take?"

"If I can have access to the office day and night, probably less than a week. If I can only work while you're here, it'll take longer. You won't like being around during the sanding or varnishing, believe me."

She reached for the scratch paper he held out to her. "Wow. Is that all? I'm amazed. Okay. Let's do it."

"Don't you have to get approval from higher up?" Trevor asked, frowning.

"Actually, this is one of the perks of being a Kessler. If I don't exceed my budget, I can do whatever I please."

"Okay. I'll write up a formal agreement for you to sign and bring it with me when I come back this afternoon. Might as well get started while I'm waiting for some back-ordered materials for another job."

"You won't quit halfway through my bookcases

and leave a mess, will you? I really need my office. The new quarter starts soon."

"No, I won't quit until this job is finished. When I make a commitment, I keep it. You can count on me."

When Steff sobered and quietly said, "I know," the sound of her voice and the suddenly charged atmosphere within the cramped office made the hair at the nape of his neck stand on end.

It looked as though working when she wasn't present was going to be more than advantageous, it was going to be critical. Especially if he hoped to finish the job and also keep what little was left of his sanity.

Stephanie had cleaned off her desk and draped a sheet of plastic over her computer station by the time Trevor returned.

"Do you want me to get lost or stay here?" she asked. "I'm curious to see what it looks like inside a wall, if you don't think I'll be in the way."

"Suit yourself. Just don't breathe the dust. I remember you used to have allergies."

"I still do."

"Then you'd better wear a disposable mask so you don't sneeze yourself to death. There are extras in my toolbox. Help yourself. And hand me one, too, will you?"

He began spreading a tarp on the floor. "I doubt this will be very interesting. About all I usually find is abandoned wasp nests and dead mice."

"Terrific."

"Don't worry. I'll protect you from the vermin. That's what this tarp is for, to catch all the dirt."

He put on one of the masks, took a pry bar and popped the baseboard off as if it were a toothpick. The wall itself proved more stubborn. Finally, he worked an opening large enough for a handhold, grabbed the plasterboard and gave it a yank. White powder filled the nearby air and made a cloud around his head.

Stephanie retreated. She'd never noticed how cramped her office was until she'd been shut in there with Trevor. She would have left then if he hadn't had to close the door to gain access to the wall he was demolishing.

Trapped by circumstances she should knew she should have considered earlier, she waved her hands. "Phew! You weren't kidding, were you?"

"I never kid about my work. You okay?"

"I suppose so." It seemed a waste of time to just stand here and watch so she began to relieve him of the small, flat pieces of chalky board as he broke them loose. If Trevor was surprised, he gave no indication of it, although she suspected he might be grinning behind his mask.

"Where shall I pile all this trash?" she asked.

"Any place out of my way. Just keep it on the tarp. It'll make cleanup easier."

"Right." She had dragged several slivers of board aside and was lifting a larger one when she stopped. "Trevor?"

Sweating in spite of the air-conditioning, he swiveled in her direction. "What? Did you find a dead mouse?"

"No. I don't know what this is. It looks like writing of some sort." Steff steadied the board fragment with one hand and used the other to brush away the powdery dust. "Do you think it's important?"

"I doubt it. One of the men who built the original wall probably drew his initials for fun. My guys do it all the time. You know, like the old 'Kilroy was here' notes the soldiers used to leave during World War II. It's nothing."

"Are you sure? I mean, I'd like to be positive. It looks to me as if it was written by a small finger dipped in something. And look. Are these spatters of blood?"

"What?"

"Never mind. I don't know why I said that. I guess these drops at the edges reminded me of blood."

"Your imagination is working overtime, that's all."

"I suppose so." Her brow knit as she studied her find. "Do you think this initial was meant to be a P or an R?"

He leaned closer and squinted. "Can't tell. The way it kind of trails off at the end it could be either."

"I know. I suppose we should notify the police, just in case, but my father is friends with the chief and if it winds up to be nothing important, as you say, I'll never hear the end of it."

"Plus, if there's an investigation, your office may look like this for weeks or maybe even months while they poke around."

"I hadn't thought of that."

"It's happened to construction projects more times than I care to remember," Trevor said. "Now, forget that piece of trash and let me do my job. Okay?"

"Okay." She pulled a face. "I know it's foolish to cause a stir, especially since my father already acts as if he thinks he's the only one capable of logical reasoning. I've been trying to prove myself to him since he first helped me get this job and I'm beginning to wonder if I'll ever succeed."

Trevor turned away to hide his reaction. Stephanie didn't make any bones about the fact she'd been born with a silver spoon in her mouth. Even now that they were both in their thirties, nothing had really changed between them. They might be professionals in their respective fields but he was still blue collar and she was still acting the part of royalty, a part she'd been born and raised to play. That was what had caused him to start teasing her by calling her Princess in the first place, back when she and his sister had been college roommates.

He gave a long, loud sigh. "Look, *Princess,* you do whatever you want with that old piece of plasterboard. Keep it or junk it or tie a ribbon around it and give it to Daddy as a gift. I couldn't care less."

"Don't be absurd." Steff rolled her eyes and arched her brows. "I told you, I have no intention of involving my father."

Backing off, she studied the scrawled letter, then began to sort through the other rubble to see if she could find more writing. That one letter and its accompanying splatter seemed to be all there was, which was probably a good sign.

Now that she'd had time to think about it she

supposed the marks could just as easily have been made with mud or paint or even chocolate, as dark brown as they were. Why she had assumed it might be blood puzzled her. Maybe she'd been reading too many mystery and suspense stories lately.

Of course. That had to be the reason. There was no need to preserve the board. After all, that wall had been built ages ago and if there had been any mayhem committed on campus her family would have known about it. Plenty of tales concerning the founding and growth of Magnolia College had been told and retold so often that she was sick of hearing them. None had involved bodily injury, unless a few broken bones on the football field counted.

She stared at the board fragment one more time, shivered slightly, then laid it on the pile of refuse with all the others.

There was nothing important or ominous about the initial. There couldn't be. Magnolia College was a safe haven and always had been. She'd stake her life on it.

The frightening incident prior to the reunion gala flashed into her mind and made her reconsider. She'd been unusually jumpy ever since that night and nothing she did seemed to erase her lingering, prickling sense of dread.

* * *

The more Trevor thought about Steff's notion that the letter scrawled inside the wall might have a sinister origin, the more the whole idea bothered him. It was probably ridiculous to take her suggestion seriously, but if he didn't at least look into the possibility of foul play, he'd always wonder. Once he had a chance to sort through the rubble in private, he'd locate the supposedly bloody writing and put it aside until he could decide what to do with it—if anything. If he did take it to the cops, not only might the job be stopped, he might also have to tear up more of Steff's office looking for further clues. And for what? A silly suspicion of foul play? The idea was ludicrous.

He made several trips out to a Dumpster he'd placed nearby for construction waste, then began to roll up the tarp containing the bulk of the chalky dust.

"Can I help you with that?" Steff asked.

Trevor laughed as he eyed her. "I think your main job should be cleaning yourself up. You're a mess, Princess."

"I wouldn't talk if I were you." She dusted her hands together before she took off her mask and handed it to him. "At least I'm a blond to start with. Your dark hair is practically white."

"I probably turned gray because you were trying to help me," Trevor quipped. He was growing more and more aware that they were both beginning to engage in the witty verbal sparring that had been such a big part of their relationship many years ago and it pleased him.

"Oh, thanks a lot. I sacrifice my manicure for you and what do I get? Sarcasm."

"Sorry about your nail polish. You should have taken my advice and stood back where you weren't in the way."

"I wasn't in the way. Even if you're not willing to admit it, I helped you a lot."

"Yes, you did." He laughed. "But that doesn't mean I'm offering you a job on one of my crews."

"I don't need another job. I have plenty to do already," Steff replied. Looking at her dust-coated desk and chair she shook her head and sighed. "I knew remodeling would be messy but I had no idea it would be this bad."

"I warned you."

"Yes, you did. I thought just putting my files away, clearing off my desk and covering my computer would suffice, but I can see I underestimated the problem." She started brushing off her slacks, then stopped. "I'm just making things worse. I'd better go outside to do this. Excuse me?"

As she sidled past, Trevor gave her as much room as possible and finished gathering up the folded tarp. It amused him to see the perfect Ms. Stephanie Kessler as dirty as a common worker, yet, even covered with dust, she was elegant and graceful.

"Get a grip, Whittaker," he muttered to himself. "You have no business even noticing that woman, let alone wasting energy thinking about her."

For the first time since he'd accepted this job he wondered if it was actually a gift from God or a test of his faith instead. He supposed it could be either, or even both, although at that moment it felt more like a big, big mistake than anything else.

Steff rejoined Trevor as he disposed of the last of the refuse. "In case I haven't already said so, thanks for agreeing to do my little job," she said. "I know it's too small to be worth much to you and I do appreciate it."

"No problem. My sister would have had my hide if I'd turned you down."

She stifled her urge to snap at him. Not only did Southern manners preclude taking offense at his implication, her pride refused to allow her to express hurt feelings.

"Then I shall definitely have to thank Alicia," she said sweetly.

If Trevor sensed anything insincere in Steff's words he gave no indication of it. "You'd better get whatever you need moved out of your office before tomorrow morning," he said. "I intend to start back to work very early."

"Then you'll want keys to the building. I have an extra set in my desk, but…"

"But what?"

"I need to ask you something first. It's been bothering me ever since the night of the reunion. It's about your shoes."

"My shoes?" He began to scowl. "I rented the monkey suit so Alicia wouldn't be embarrassed. Wasn't I well-dressed enough for you, Princess?"

"It's not that. It was the mud on your heel." She hesitated, nervous, then blurted, "Were you poking around outside the library earlier in the evening?"

"Me?" Trevor's frown deepened. "No. Of course not. Ask Alicia. She was with me the whole time."

"I won't need to ask anyone else. Your word is good enough for me. Wait here. I'll be right back."

When she returned, he thanked her for the keys,

then climbed into his pickup and drove away without further small talk.

Steff stood in the shade of the oaks and watched him disappear into the distance. What was it about Trevor that made her feel so unsure of herself? He was the only person she knew who could fluster her all the way to her toes, the only one who could rattle her with a simple arch of his eyebrow.

And those dark, brooding eyes. She took a deep breath and released it as a sigh, relieved that he hadn't been the man she'd encountered near the library.

Penitent, she realized she should have known that without asking. Granted, when Trevor looked at her she still got the same chills she'd felt when she was in her late teens, but there was nothing malicious or frightening in his gaze. Quite the contrary.

Nevertheless, she was grateful for her ability to hide her innermost feelings, to behave as if she didn't care what he, or anyone else, thought of her.

The only thing better would be if it were true.

THREE

Trevor ended up at Burt's Pizza for supper. The brick oven pizzeria on Main Street had been a local hangout for as long as he could recall and stepping inside always reminded him of his college days.

His favorite booth in the back corner had been removed but Trevor could still picture the cracked, red, leatherlike seats and the marred tabletop. He had never taken Steff anywhere on a date but he had managed to catch her and Alicia at Burt's quite often.

He'd sauntered up to their booth one day, years ago, when he'd spotted them dining there. Giving his best impression of a notorious bad boy, he had been greeted by an exaggerated roll of Steff's beautiful eyes.

"Look what the cat dragged in," she had drawled.

Trevor remembered giving her a lazy smile.

"Hello to you, too, Princess. Are y'all holding court or can a commoner like me join you?"

Alicia had quickly scooted over to make room for him. "We have a slice of pepperoni left, if you're hungry."

"No thanks. Save it for the princess. She looks like she could use a square meal. A guy could get bruised trying to hug her."

"That will never be a problem for you," Steff had countered. She'd arched an eyebrow and given him a disparaging once-over. "It's a good thing for you Burt doesn't have a dress code. Those worn-out jeans are really disgusting. You look like a bum."

"Oh? And how would you know? Do you know any bums?" The moment he'd said it he'd realized he'd left himself open to a witty retort. Steff didn't miss the chance to take another clever jab at him, either.

"Only you," she had said, smiling sweetly. "But bless your heart, I don't think you have a clue how disgusting you look."

Recalling the exchange, Trevor had to smile in spite of himself. He'd been positive, until very recently, that the Lord was simply using him to help his family, but now that he'd spent more time around Steff he was beginning to wonder more and more often what else might be going on. Visions of her and memories of their relationship in the old days kept popping into his mind.

Trevor quickly and flatly denied that Steff had any place in his life other than as his sister's friend. The best thing he could do was finish the bookcases in her office and distance himself from the entire situation as soon as possible.

Thirteen or fourteen years ago he'd have boxed up his pizza and hauled it over to Alicia's dorm room at Edith Sutton Hall to share with her and Steff. There wasn't much about his rowdy, younger years that he missed except that kind of casual socializing.

And now? Trevor shook his head. Nothing had changed except that he was a lot older and hopefully much, much wiser. He was still a blue jeans kind of guy and he wasn't about to change his ways for anyone, especially not stuffy Ms. Stephanie Kessler. As a matter of fact, when he got home he was going to dig out the most worn pair of jeans he had and wear them when he went to work on her office in the morning, just to make that very point.

And when she objected this time he was going to thoroughly enjoy rebutting her protest. If there was one thing he and Steff loved to do, it was turn their innate differences into reasons to exchange clever barbs. He supposed, to an outsider, their war of words might sound like a real argument but he knew better. Steff loved matching wits with him as much as he loved going head-to-head with her. Theirs was a contest that had been going on since they'd first met and as yet had produced no clear winner.

Trevor smiled to himself. If the time ever came that Steff was too nice to him, that was when he'd start to worry.

Steff was restless. She'd tried drinking warm milk and had gone to bed early but relaxation and sleep had eluded her. Disgusted, she pulled on a pair of designer jeans and an embroidered sweatshirt, grabbed her purse and headed back to campus.

Although she wasn't fond of poking around alone in the dark, especially since the night of the reunion, she wasn't certain when Trevor's special Dumpster would be emptied and she didn't want the scrap of board with the initial to disappear before she'd had another chance to at least study it.

Arriving, she angled her car so its headlights illuminated the Dumpster and helped dispel the shadows that continued to make her so jumpy. She carried a chair from the foyer of the Administration building so she'd have something to stand on, placed it against the trash bin and climbed up.

The headlights on her left were blinding yet failed to illuminate the depths. Her only recourse was to start lifting pieces of board out of the way and dropping them on the ground until she'd dug down to the one she was looking for.

"My mother would disown me if she saw me doing this," Steff told herself with a wry chuckle. "Kesslers do *not* Dumpster dive."

Piece after piece of wallboard fell at the foot of her chair and still she hadn't located the initial. She paused, confused and sneezing from the dust she'd raised. The disturbing piece of board had been a good-size, she recalled, so how could she have overlooked it?

Perhaps Trevor had broken up the larger sections as he'd thrown them away. She huffed in disgust. If that was the case, there was no telling what had become of the remnant. It might have been totally destroyed.

Steff had to lean further and further in to reach the scraps. She was so intent on her search she failed to hear someone approaching.

When a deep voice behind her asked, "What are

you doing?" she almost lost her balance and fell headfirst into the trash container.

Her, "What?" came out more as a scream than a word.

"Look out," the man shouted as he grabbed her ankle.

His touch panicked her. She levered herself up and whirled as she shot out of the bin, almost losing her balance and tumbling off the chair into his arms.

Eyes wide, she shrieked, "Let me go!"

The middle-aged man backed off, his hands raised in surrender. "I'm sorry, Stephanie. I didn't recognize you. What in the world are you doing here at this time of night?"

It took a few seconds for Steff to realize she knew him. Her hands flew to her throat as she fought to catch her breath. "Oh, Professor Rutherford, it's you. You gave me an awful scare!"

"I've told you to call me Cornell," he said kindly.

"Sorry." She managed a smile although her heart was still threatening to pound out of her ribs. "Actually, I should I apologize for not calling you *Dean* Rutherford now that you're head of the Liberal Arts department. I guess I still feel like your student. Your classes were always favorites of mine."

"Thank you. I enjoyed teaching you, too." He

was smiling benevolently. "Now, suppose you tell me what you're doing."

"It's a long story. I was looking for a piece of old wall from my office."

"Why on earth would you do that?"

"There was an initial drawn on it and some splattered droplets that might be blood. The more I got to thinking about it, the more I wanted to see it again just to make sure. I guess my imagination was working overtime." She paused for a sigh and a quick sneeze. "Anyway, it's a moot point because I can't find the piece again."

"It was in this Dumpster?"

"Yes. At least, I thought it was." Eyeing the pile of scraps on the ground, she shrugged. "I guess it's lost forever."

Rutherford had shed his nylon windbreaker and laid it aside on the well-manicured lawn. "If it bothers you that much, we should search until we find it. What did it look like? How big was it?"

She held her hands a foot apart. "About like this, although Trevor may have broken it into smaller chunks when he threw it away. The initial itself was four or five inches high. We couldn't tell if it was supposed to be a messy P or an R. Or neither."

Hesitating a moment, the dean took her place at

the side of the Dumpster. "All right. I'll throw out everything at least that big and you can look over each piece before we put it back in."

"You don't have to do that," Steff argued. "I feel foolish for even worrying about it."

"Nonsense. I won't have you fretting."

"That's really nice of you."

In the next breath she nearly gasped. Dean Rutherford was crawling into that filthy trash bin. In all the time she'd known him she'd never seen him even get his hands dirty, let alone risk damaging his fashionable clothing, although she supposed the more casual attire he had on tonight wasn't as expensive as the silk suits he normally sported.

He's doing it because I'm a Kessler and he wants to stay on my family's good side, Steff deduced. After all, he was also married to a Kessler cousin, so he certainly knew how influential the family was. She pulled a face. This wasn't the first time members of the college staff had given her preferential treatment because of her prominent family and it probably wouldn't be the last, either.

Disgruntled, she waited until the Dumpster was empty, then began sorting through the scraps while the dean stood back and watched. To her dismay, the clue wasn't there. The poor man had sacrificed his fine clothes for nothing.

Maybe, in the long run, it was all for the best, she concluded with a sigh. If there had been real blood on the scrap she'd not only have had a better reason to continue to be apprehensive, she'd probably feel the need to notify the police, and her father would surely hear of it.

Considering the way she'd been reacting to the slightest unusual occurrence lately, Steff didn't need to add any more confusion or look for any other reasons to be afraid. She was already more jumpy and upset than she'd been since the days following her eldest brother Adam's untimely death.

It had been ten years since that horrible summer day, yet there were times, like now, when the sense of tragedy was so strong she felt as if she were losing dear sweet Adam all over again.

Steff had moved herself into a coworker's office for the time that her own work space was off-limits. She'd cleared a corner of her friend Brenda's desk to make room for her laptop and had pulled up a side chair. That arrangement was decidedly uncomfortable.

Stretching, she stood and rubbed the small of

her back. "I need to move around before I stiffen up any more. I'm going to run down to the basement for a few minutes."

"What for?" Brenda's brown eyes narrowed. "It's dark and dingy and spooky down there. You wouldn't get me to go alone if you paid me."

"We do pay you," Steff teased. "But don't worry. I won't make you do anything like that. I just want to see if I can find some old blueprints and maybe some contracts for those earlier projects."

"Why?"

"Curiosity," Steff replied, thinking mainly of the intriguing initial she'd noticed then lost track of. Maybe, if she could learn more about the original construction of that wall, she'd be able to put her concerns to rest. It was worth a try. "I'll need some of the old plans eventually anyway, when we get closer to building the library annex. And I want to see if I can figure out when some prior construction was done on my office, too."

"Okay. It's your funeral."

Steff gave a nervous laugh and made light of the comment as she left the office. "I sure hope not!"

However, the spring in her step diminished as she approached the doorway that led to the basement stairs. Brenda's suggestion that the cavernous storage area was frightening was ridiculous. So why was the hair on the back of her neck prickling?

"Because my imagination is working overtime again. I really should have been a mystery writer," Steff said to herself wryly. Maybe someday she'd pursue that dream and give fiction writing a try. Right now, Magnolia College needed her and she was going to continue to support her alma mater for as long as that was true. And perhaps, in doing so, she could favorably impress her parents—especially her father.

"Ha! That'll be the day," Steff muttered, disgusted to have even entertained the thought.

She flipped on a light at the top of the narrow stairs and paused for a moment to gather her courage. Filled with trepidation but determined to ignore it, she started slowly down, her hand sliding along the smoothly worn handrail.

This part of the college had been converted into offices after serving for years as a dorm, and the basement showed its age. Heavy, dark beams supported the ceiling and the rough rock of the interior walls was not plastered. Small windows at ground level didn't let in much natural light because of the evergreen foundation planting of azaleas and stocky palmettos.

As Steff reached the bottom of the stairs she hesitated. Something was amiss. A frown creased her brow. She hadn't been downstairs in ages but she didn't recall the archives being such a cluttered mess. What in the world could have happened to them? And why?

The oblong tubes containing blueprints were easy to locate because of their unusual shape. The other paperwork was not. A thick layer of dust had been disturbed where the bank records were stored, making her suspect that the boxes had recently been moved and perhaps opened.

Puzzled, she stood quietly and stared while her mind raced. In the background a mouse skittered. The beams overhead creaked. Something rustled in a far corner.

The hair on Steff's neck began to prickle in earnest. She had just started to turn back toward the stairs when she thought she glimpsed movement in the shadows.

She froze. Was she imagining things? Probably. After all, she and Brenda were the only ones upstairs right now, so there couldn't be anyone else in the basement.

Except Trevor, she added, since he was supposed to be working in her office.

Steff's survival instincts took over. She grabbed the blueprints she'd come for, whirled and dashed toward the stairway at a run.

At this point it didn't matter whether there was a prowler lurking behind her in the darkness or not. All she wanted was to escape!

Trevor was carrying another wooden plank through the foyer when a breathless, wide-eyed Stephanie crested the stairs. He dropped the board and ran to her as soon as he saw her panicky expression.

"What is it? What's the matter?"

"Nothing," she insisted, fighting to catch her breath.

He grasped her shoulders and held her fast. "Don't give me that. You're shaking like a leaf. What's wrong?"

"I, um, I thought I heard somebody in the basement just now. Brenda was giving me spooky ideas and I know my imagination took over. It can't be anything."

"Suppose I go take a look."

"That's not necessary."

"Maybe not. But I'm going to do it anyway. You coming?"

Steff shook her head and hung back. "That's okay. I'll wait here."

"Suit yourself." He pushed through the door and descended the staircase a lot faster than she had.

She stood in the open doorway and called down, "Do you see anything?"

"Not yet."

Trevor began to systematically search the stacks. It wasn't until he came to the farthest overhead window that he began to think Steff may have actually sensed something amiss. The hinged pane wasn't all the way open but it wasn't latched, either. There was a remote possibility that someone athletic enough to pull himself up and wriggle through could have left by that route. Of course, the basement denizen could just as easily have been one of the pet campus cats. That was a much more likely scenario.

Trevor closed and secured the window, then returned to Steff. "There's nobody down there now, but I did find one window half open. I closed and latched it for you. Whoever or whatever it was can't get back in now, so the problem is solved." He hesitated, unsure about her steadiness. "You okay?"

"I told you, I'm fine."

"Then you might want to stop shaking." For the first time he took notice of the armload of material she was carrying. "What have you got there?"

"Blueprints," Steff said. "I'm sure you've heard that we're going to add on to the Kessler Library. I wanted to see the original plans."

"No, I hadn't heard. When were you going to tell me about it? After the contract was done and it was too late for Whittaker Construction to bid?"

"Of course not. The job will be advertised, as always," Steff said firmly. "As a privately funded college we don't have to do that, you know, but we always try to be fair."

"Oh, sure. You hand me the crumbs so Alicia will think you're on our side, then award the really plum job to somebody else. Which company has the inside track, Steff? Is it Fowler Brothers? I know they're tight with your father."

She bristled in response to his accusatory tone. "Nobody has any inside tracks, Mr. Whittaker."

"We'll see about that. I'll be finished in your office in a few more days, but I'll be watching the newspapers for the official the announcement. When the bids come in, Whittaker Construction's will be included."

"I know the board of trustees will look forward

to considering it," she said formally. "Now, if you'll excuse me."

He stepped aside and watched her walk stiffly away, her heels clicking on the inlaid hardwood floor. Disgusted with himself for snapping at her, he stomped over to the board he'd dropped and picked it up. The way he was feeling right now, Trevor figured he could gnaw that board to size about as fast as he could saw it with his power tools.

He hadn't meant to antagonize Steff. On the contrary, he was deeply concerned about her, which may have been why he'd reacted as strongly as he had. He knew she was hiding something and he didn't appreciate being kept in the dark.

Like it or not, Steff and he were emotionally connected. His dilemma was not whether to acknowledge his newfound empathy. It was figuring out how to deal with it.

FOUR

Steff's cell phone rang later in the day. To her chagrin the caller was her father, J. T. Kessler.

"Stephanie," he said, sounding as blunt as always.

"Hello, Dad."

Instead of pleasantries, J.T. launched into a tirade. "I heard you hired that Whittaker firm. What were you thinking?"

"They're building a bookcase in my office. I hardly think that's earth-shattering. Besides, I have discretion about small jobs. You said so yourself."

"That was when I thought you were halfway intelligent."

Steff could hear her mother's voice in the background, wheedling as if she were trying to calm him down.

"Well, what do you have to say for yourself, young lady?" J.T. insisted.

Rather than waste her breath arguing, Steff simply gripped the phone tighter and said, "I'm thirty-two years old, I have a degree in business administration, seven years experience in my job and almost perfect yearly evaluations. What do you expect me to say, Dad?"

"You might try a little penitence."

"Not when it's not warranted," she said flatly. "Alicia has moved back to Magnolia Falls and Trevor is helping his father run Whittaker Construction. I see no reason not to give him a chance to prove his skill."

She was relieved when her father finally said, "Very well," though not comforted when he hung up without bidding her a polite goodbye.

She sighed. So much for impressing her parents. Thank goodness she hadn't involved the local police in her silly worries about the initial she'd found hidden in the wall! She could just imagine what a ranting she'd have had to listen to from her father if she'd done that.

She couldn't really understand why she seemed to never measure up to her parents' impossible ideals the way her late brother Adam once had. She was the one supporting the college and carrying on the Kessler tradition at Magnolia, yet her surviving brother, Luke, got all the praise. Why couldn't her parents see how hard she was trying to please them?

When she turned around, Trevor was standing in the doorway behind her.

"I'm sorry," he said.

"For what? For accusing me of favoritism?"

"Yes. And no. I'm sorry I didn't realize you'd stuck your neck out to offer me this job in the first place."

"It's no big deal."

"It is to me," he said quietly. "I'm taking a break and I'm thirsty. Do you have any sweet tea around here?"

"If Brenda didn't drink it all, I do." She stood and started toward him. "About-face. It's in the break room."

"After you, Miss Stephanie."

She smiled as she passed him. "When you call me that you make me feel like somebody's grandmother. I prefer to reserve that kind of polite endearment for elderly ladies."

Trevor chuckled. "Okay. No more Miss Stephanie. I like Steff better anyway. It's less formal."

"That's probably why my parents refuse to use it," she said over her shoulder. "Just one more reason to scold me."

"I gathered J.T. was reading you the riot act about hiring me."

"Hey, if it wasn't that, it would be something else. I never have been able to please Dad. That's just how it is. Unfortunately, I'm not perfect."

"You don't have to be perfect, Steff. Not for your friends." He closed the distance between them as they entered the break room. "And especially not for God. If He required that His children be perfect to be acceptable to Him, none of us would make it. Which reminds me."

"Uh-oh. You sound serious. Should I run?"

Trevor laughed. "No. I just remembered that Alicia needs help several evenings next week for VBS. Maybe you could volunteer."

"For *what?*"

"Vacation Bible School. She made the mistake of offering her services and they put her in charge of snacks."

"I never bake cookies," Steff replied.

"You wouldn't have to. All you'd have to do is pour punch and hand out the cookies. You can handle that, can't you?" He grinned. "It would really help Alicia. I know she needs more willing workers."

"Willing? Well, that lets me out," Steff quipped.

She raised her eyebrows and looked at him askance. "Are you going to be there, too?"

"Yes, but only as a temporary teacher. They roped me into taking the class of six-year-olds because I'm used to watching my sister's kids. I'll be lucky if I survive."

His candor made her laugh lightly. "I'll think about it, okay? I'm not much for churchgoing."

"Why not?"

She shrugged, feeling a little ill at ease. "I don't know. Probably because I never saw the need. My parents went to church regularly, though. Dad spent his time looking for business prospects and Mom went to show off her jewelry and fancy clothes. As soon as I was brave enough to speak for myself, I stopped going with them."

"That's not what it's all about," Trevor said. There was a warmth, a gentleness, in his gaze that made her tremble.

All she added before purposely changing the subject was "If you say so."

Steff was glad for the diversion of the monthly potluck supper she and some of her college friends had started again after the reunion. Although she was so emotionally frazzled from being near

Trevor and from all the strange goings-on at work, she wished it wasn't her turn to host it.

Looking around her pristine condo, she was thankful the cleaning staff had done such a good job, not that her home was ever messy. Unlike the grandeur and almost-Victorian decor of her parents' mansion, her condo was simply furnished in mostly off-white and pale shades of mauve, and displayed the reserved elegance she preferred.

If Trevor ever saw the place he'd probably tell her it was too neat, she mused, although Alicia hadn't said anything derogatory when she'd stopped by a week or so ago.

The doorbell chimed. Steff smoothed her bejeweled T-shirt over the hips of her designer jeans and went to answer.

"Cassie! Jennifer!" she said with a grin. "Come in, come in. You're the first ones here."

Cassie headed straight for the kitchen. "I made a soufflé but it fell, so I stopped to get a pizza. Hope you don't mind?"

"Not at all," Steff said. "Actually, I picked up a quiche from the Mossy Oak Inn on my way home."

"That's our Steff," Jennifer teased. "Always first-class. You'll have us spoiled yet."

"Yeah," Cassie added with a giggle.

Steff made a silly face. "Knock it off, you two. I only went to the inn because it's so close to my office."

"All I brought was a salad, and it's a good thing," Jennifer said. "I had car trouble and Cassie had to give me a ride over. Is Kate coming?"

"Far as I know. I invited Alicia, too. I hope y'all don't mind."

"Not us," Cassie said with a sly smile. "You have to keep Trevor's baby sister happy, right?"

Steff took a playful swipe at her outspoken friend. "I asked Alicia because she's been too busy to connect very well since she moved back to Magnolia Falls."

"Right. And her handsome brother has nothing to do with it."

"That's right." Steff did her best to stifle a silly grin that kept trying to lift the corners of her mouth. "Besides, I see plenty of Trevor at work. I told you I'd hired him to remodel my office, didn't I?"

"You certainly did. Several times," Cassie teased. "How's that going, anyway?"

"Just fine." Remembering the initial and dabs of what had looked like blood that she and Trevor had found hidden in the office wall, Steff grew solemn and added, "For the most part."

"Uh-oh."

She waved her hands in dismissal. "No, no. It was nothing, really. We just…" She hesitated. "Never mind."

Both her friends leaned closer, eager to hear more. "No way," Jennifer said. "You can't start a story and stop in the middle like that. What happened? Did he make a pass at you or something?"

"Of course not! We found a funny thing inside the wall, that's all."

"Like what?"

"Yeah, like what?"

Steff took a deep breath and exhaled slowly. "It was an initial. Somebody drew the letter P or R on the inside of the wallboard. It looked as if it was written by a finger dipped in something. And there were drops of what looked like blood splattered around near the outer edge of the piece, too."

"Eeew." Cassie made a face. "As my students would say, that's totally gross."

"I agree. But Trevor wasn't at all concerned, so we threw it away. I really wish we hadn't."

"What? You didn't give it to the police? Why not?"

"It's a long story."

The doorbell sounded again before Steff could elaborate and she hurried to answer. "Alicia! Come in. I was just telling Cassie and Jennifer that I'd invited you." Steff guided her through the living room to the kitchen. "You can put your casserole on top of the stove. I want to give Kate a few more minutes to get here before we eat."

"Fine." Alicia smiled at the others. "So, what's new with y'all?"

Cassie answered. "Actually, Steff was just telling us about something weird she found in her office wall."

"You mean, the initial?"

Steff frowned, puzzled. "Trevor mentioned it to you?"

"No. I saw it and asked him about it."

"You *saw* it? When? How?"

"He brought it home with him. Why?"

Steff was astounded. "I can't believe this. He insisted it was *nothing*." She scowled as she recalled her late-night efforts to recover the clue that Trevor had already saved. "He lied to me."

"I wouldn't go that far," Alicia said. "He probably just didn't want you to worry."

"Humph. I'm a lot more concerned now than I

was before. I can hardly wait till I see him tomorrow."

"Uh-oh," Cassie quipped. "The fat's in the fire now."

Everyone else had had to leave earlier so Steff offered to drive Jennifer home. It was a balmy summer night and pleasant being outside.

Seated beside her, Jennifer ran her hand over the smooth leather upholstery. "Nice car, Steff."

"Thanks. It was a present—from me to myself."

"Good for you. I'm still driving the old clunker I had when we graduated."

"No wonder it didn't want to start," Steff joked. "The poor thing is tired."

Jennifer leaned her head back against the seat and sighed. "Mmm-hmm. Me, too. I know I'm doing the right thing by running the nursery and after-school programs at the church, but it is tiring. I can certainly understand why people like Kate and Alicia say they're glad they had their children while they were younger."

"You and I are not exactly ancient," Steff countered. "I think establishing a career first is very important."

"I'm not so sure. When I'm looking after those little ones all day, they really get to me."

"Make you notice your biological clock, you mean?"

"Something like that. Then again, there is a lot to be said for not rushing things the way Penny and Adam did." She glanced at Steff. "Sorry. I didn't mean to bring up old hurts."

"It's okay." Steff managed to force a smile she hoped looked natural. "My brother's been gone a long time."

"Do you ever wonder about Penny? I mean, don't your parents want to know what's become of her and their only grandchild."

"They might if they believed Alexis was really Adam's daughter," Steff said. "Penny showed up at my folks' estate after the baby was born, acting as though she expected to be welcomed with open arms in spite of all the nasty things she'd said to us at Adam's funeral."

"Oh, dear. How awful."

Steff's hands tightened on the steering wheel, her knuckles whitening. "That's an understatement. Dad said he wanted Penny to have the baby's DNA tested. It seemed like a sensible request to me, but Penny refused to even consider it. When

Dad insisted, she got furious. By then my mother was in tears. It was awful."

"Haven't they seen the little girl since she was a baby?"

"No. None of us have."

"What about child support? Adam and Penny were married, right? Isn't his estate financially responsible?"

"I suppose it would be if Penny chose to press the issue. I tried to locate her to invite her to our class reunion but wherever she is, she's doing a good job of hiding."

"Do you think she's actually hiding?"

"Not literally," Steff said with a quick shake of her head. "I think poor Penny just burned all her bridges around here and went somewhere where no one knows about her messy past. I can't imagine being so emotionally off balance over a man that I'd compromise my standards to make him marry me the way she did to Adam."

Jennifer giggled. "You've never been in love, have you?"

"Sure, I have. Remember Luke's friend, John? We dated for a long time. He even asked me to marry him."

"Why didn't you?"

"My parents pushed so hard to convince me, I wouldn't have given in if he'd been the last available man in Magnolia Falls."

"Then you didn't really love him," Jennifer said. "If you had, nothing could have stopped you, not even outside interference."

Steff shrugged as she pulled up to the curb in front of Jennifer's house. "Well, I'm certainly never going to put myself into an untenable position the way Adam did. I can't believe he was really happy, but it was his choice to make, not mine. I'm just sorry he didn't live long enough to work out the glitches in his marriage."

Climbing out, Jennifer reached for her empty salad bowl then paused at the open passenger door. "Me, too. Thanks for inviting us again. Good night."

"'Night."

Steff watched until her old friend reached the door and safely let herself in before she pulled away from the curb. It always hurt to talk about Adam, but she supposed doing so was good for her. His death was something she'd had to accept, just as she accepted that the sun rose each morning and set each evening. It simply was. There was no discussion or argument that could change that fact, nor was yearning for him going to alter anything that had happened in the past.

She knew, without hearing the actual words, that her parents often wished she had been the one to perish in that boating accident instead of their eldest, most beloved son.

Chin held high, Steff blinked back unshed tears. It would be nice to think that Trevor had been right when he'd told her that God loved her just as she was, that she was acceptable to her heavenly Father, even though her earthly one seemed constantly disappointed in her.

For the first time in longer than she could recall, she tried to pray. There were no fancy phrases embellishing her wordless plea, just a heartfelt need, and in reply she received peace that flowed over her like warm oil, anointing her all the way to her tender soul.

The unexpected phenomenon surprised her so much her jaw dropped. She blinked to try to clear her head. What had just occurred? How could it logically be explained?

"I finally relaxed, that's all," she concluded. "I've been tense ever since I hired Trevor, anyway, and with all the talk about Adam, I was simply overwrought."

Sure, that was it. After all, she might believe in God in a basic way but she was far from buying into the theory that He cared about inconsequential things.

"Like me," she added with self-deprecation. It was a relief to feel better but she wasn't willing to attribute her lift to anything spiritual.

Steff knew she had no one she could depend upon one hundred percent but herself. She'd learned that lesson long ago. She was strong, self-reliant, smart, capable and successful at whatever she made up her mind to do. She didn't need anyone or anything else. Or did she?

Her thoughts flashed back to the night of the reunion, then quickly progressed to her fright in the basement. Okay, so maybe there had been a couple of times lately when she'd wished she'd had backup. That didn't changed the fact that she could take care of herself. Period.

She believed that wholeheartedly, so why was her stomach continually churning and why did she so often feel anxious?

"Trevor," she answered immediately, and this time she didn't bother to argue. He didn't scare her, not the way the man lurking next to the library had, but he didn't help her feel very settled or secure, either. Especially not since she'd found out he'd been lying to her.

FIVE

The more Steff thought about Trevor's subterfuge regarding the clue from the wall, the more angry she became. Rather than drive directly home from Jennifer's she detoured past the Magnolia campus to see if he was still working. Judging by the looks of the Administration building, he was.

She proceeded down the narrow, winding, oak-lined road, parked her Mercedes next to Trevor's truck and hurried up the walk. He had the building's doors propped open and the overhead lights were drawing moths of all sizes, some as big as hummingbirds!

Wishing that the door had a screen she could close, Steff waved the moths away and headed for her office. All the lights were on in there, too, but there was no sign of Trevor.

She was about to call his name when she noticed that the door to the basement storage area was ajar.

Frowning, thoughtful, she walked to the doorway, opened it the rest of the way and peered down into the depths. The basement lights were not lit but she could see the beam of a flashlight moving among the stacks.

This time she knew it had to be Trevor. *What could he be doing? And why not switch on the overhead lights?* Surely if he'd wanted anything from down there he'd simply have asked, particularly after the heated discussion they'd already had about it.

Then again, Trevor wasn't the type to ask permission or to tell anyone what he was doing, especially if he wasn't certain his ideas would be well received. He never had been, which was one reason he'd gotten into so much trouble in his youth.

His practice of keeping secrets was the reason she was so upset with him at present, she reminded herself.

Determined to face him and give him the reprimand he deserved, Steff started down the cellar stairs without hesitation. If Trevor thought he was going to get the best of the other construction companies by poking through the records of previous jobs, he had another think coming. Being fair meant being fair to *all* the bidders for the library job, not just Whittaker Construction.

She wasn't trying to mask the noise of her approach and her steps echoed hollowly on the wooden staircase. The beam of light had been moving behind stacks of boxes that were arranged like a library. Suddenly it went out.

Steff paused to give her eyes a chance to adjust to the dimness. Thankfully, there was still the light shining down the stairwell behind her to help her see.

"Okay, Trevor. Enough games," she said loudly. "I know you're down here so you may as well show yourself."

Nothing moved. The light remained off. Steff was beginning to have second thoughts about being down here in the semidarkness.

The short hairs at the nape of her neck tickled a warning. She tensed and her hand gripped the smooth banister as if it, alone, were keeping her standing firmly upright.

To her annoyance, her voice sounded tremulous as she demanded, "Trevor, knock it off. Trevor?"

No one answered. The silence weighed heavily on her emotions as if it were a thick, smothering blanket. Steff's muscles knotted. Her nerves tingled. The insistent urge to escape was strong enough to make her start to turn to face up the stairs.

That was a mistake. Almost immediately she was grabbed from behind and cast aside as if she were weightless.

Landing on her hands and knees, too stunned to cry out, she thought she felt something substantial brush past her.

The cement floor was icy-cold. Her palms smarted. Her heartbeats pounded in her temples and echoed in her ears. *How dare he!*

More angry than injured, she started to get to her feet just as the door at the top of the stairs slammed, leaving her in total darkness.

That changed everything.

Trevor was returning from the break room when he heard incessant pounding. Following the sound, he twisted the knob on the basement door, found it locked, and started trying Steff's spare keys until he located the right one.

He jerked the door open.

She rushed straight into his arms, nearly bowling him over, and remained there for several seconds before forcefully shoving him away.

"That wasn't funny," she declared.

"What are you talking about? How did you get stuck down there?"

"You locked me in."

"I what? Be serious, Steff. Why would I do that?"

"Because I caught you snooping around."

"Oh, really?" Trevor was fighting to control his temper. "And why would I want to do that?"

"I don't know. Maybe to get the jump on Fowler Brothers? To see what we'd paid for their previous work so you could underbid them for the library?"

"If I wanted to know what they'd charged, I'd ask them. Or you. I wouldn't have to sneak to find out."

"Are you trying to tell me you weren't messing around in the old records?"

"I'm not *trying* to tell you anything," Trevor said flatly. "I *am* telling you. I was not in the basement. And I did not lock the door on you." He gave her a look of disdain. "Whether or not you choose to believe me, that's the truth."

He could tell from her confused expression that she wasn't sure what to think. Suspecting him was natural, he guessed, since no one else was supposed to be here at this time of night. Her refusal to accept his honest denial, however, hurt his pride.

Steff smoothed the hem of her shirt over her

hips and stood ramrod-straight. "If it wasn't you, then who was it?"

"I don't know. Didn't you see?"

"No. It was dark and he surprised me."

Trevor tensed and peered into the darkness of the basement. "You're sure it was a man?" He sidled protectively between Steff and the open doorway. "Maybe he's still down there."

"I doubt it. I'm almost positive I saw a big shadow dart out the door just before I was locked in." She shivered and studied Trevor as though she was arguing with herself over whether or not to accept his alibi.

He ignored the unspoken implication. "What are you doing back here at this time of night, anyway?"

"I was just passing by and I saw the lights, so I stopped."

"Do you want me to call the police or report this incident to campus security?"

"No way. I'm already on the outs with my father. I don't need to make any more waves, thank you."

He suspected she was making excuses because she was trying to protect him. Therefore, she must still believe he was guilty. That wasn't a very comforting conclusion. "Okay, if you're sure that's how you want to handle it."

"I'm positive. No one was hurt. Besides, I could have been mistaken."

"Just the same, I'll walk you back out to your car. Are you calm enough to drive home by yourself?"

"Don't be silly. Of course I am."

Opening the driver's door, he held it as he scanned the backseat. "Looks safe enough. Lock yourself in."

Steff paused, her hands fisted on her hips. "Hold it, mister. Before I go, I have something to ask you."

He didn't like her accusatory tone or her closed expression. "Okay, shoot. But make it quick. I have hours more work to do tonight."

"Why didn't you tell me you were going to save that piece of writing we found in the wall?"

"Who says I did?" He scowled. "Never mind. I take it Alicia has been blabbing."

"She told me you kept it, yes. Do you have any idea how much trouble that caused me? I spent hours sorting through that trash trying to find it."

Trevor shrugged, hoping he looked as nonchalant as he intended. "You did? Sorry."

"When were you planning to tell me you had it?"

"I don't know. Maybe never." His hand was still on the car door, keeping Steff from storming away in a huff. He gestured with his other hand. "It's not important. Get in your car and go home. The excitement's over."

Giving him a disparaging look, she got in the car and slammed the door.

Watching her drive away, Trevor wondered if she truly believed anything he'd said. He hoped so, but he seriously doubted it.

Thoughtful, he started back into the office. If he'd been in Steff's shoes he'd probably have had the same reaction. The only things that really bothered him were not knowing who she had surprised in the storage area and why he'd been there.

Reentering the building he headed straight for the basement. If there was anyone still poking around, he was going to find him and settle things once and for all.

Trevor hoped he did encounter the prowler. At least that way he'd be able to prove to Steff that he had not been the one who had cruelly locked her in.

His fists clenched as he pictured her face, recalled the terror he'd seen in her usually lovely eyes. He wasn't violent a man but he wasn't averse to taking on anyone who abused Steff. Nobody was going to get away with harming or scaring her. Not while he was around.

Opening the door, Trevor switched on all the

overhead lights and started cautiously down the stairs. To his disappointment, although he searched every nook and cranny, there was no sign of a prowler other than a few out-of-place boxes and some disturbed dust that could have been caused by Steff herself.

As he turned to start back up the stairs he looked at the risers. The prints his work boots had left in the dust were evident from the waffling of the soles. Steff's smaller, smooth prints were easy to pick out, too, and he could see where she had stepped, both on her way down and going back up.

The hair on the back of Trevor's neck prickled. He froze. There was a third set of footprints, large like his, only with a different sole. They were man-size. And they looked as if they overlapped some of Steff's.

"What are you calling me for? I told you to leave me alone unless I contacted you."

"Something's come up. Something you should know about."

"It can't be that important."

"I wouldn't be so sure if I were you."

The recipient of the telephone call made a

sound of disgust. "All right. Tell me what's got you so upset, and it had better be good."

"Oh, it's good, all right. Remember that night about ten years ago when you had those serious problems on campus?"

"Maybe I do, maybe I don't."

"Well, you'd better think carefully. Is there any way our late, lamented friend could have left something behind on some of the construction materials that were piled outside near the library?"

"What are you talking about? I was very careful."

"I'm not so sure. It seems Ms. Kessler has come across an initial that she insists was written in blood and she's blabbing all over campus about finding it."

"*My* initial?" The voice was shrill.

"Perhaps. Perhaps not. I'm just checking."

"Well, what did it look like?"

"I don't know. She seems to have misplaced it."

"Then forget it." A sigh echoed, deep and noisy. "And unless you find it and it does implicate me, I don't want to hear from you again. When I need to deal with you, I'll be the one to initiate the call. Got that?"

"Don't forget, we're in this together."

The voice on the other end of the line laughed

hoarsely. "Sure, we are. Some of us just care more about our supposedly sterling reputations than others do. Goodbye."

Staring at the receiver, his fist tightened. Someday, hopefully, the guilty party would pay for all this. The only question he had was whether more than one person would end up taking the fall. Namely, him.

Steff relived her recent scares every time she arrived at work during the ensuing days. She didn't like being so apprehensive, not even a tiny bit, especially since she had always thought of Magnolia College as her refuge. Something had changed, starting with the prowler by the library and intensifying when she'd been locked in the basement, and she wasn't sure how to overcome her lingering misgivings.

"It's all Trevor's fault," she muttered, thinking she was alone.

Brenda's head popped around the corner from the break room. "What is? What's he done?"

Sighing deeply, Steff shook her head as she joined her coworker. "Maybe nothing. I don't know. Remember how you were scared to death of going into the basement?"

"Sure, I do. I still am. Why?"

"Well, I got locked in there a few nights ago."

"You're not serious!"

"Unfortunately, I am. It was after hours and I thought Trevor was messing around, so I went to down investigate."

Brenda's eyes widened. "Was he?"

"I don't know. He said he was in here, having a cup of coffee, when somebody knocked me down, ran up the stairs and locked the door."

"Oh, you poor thing!" She grabbed Steff's hand. "How did you get out?"

"Trevor. He said he heard me pounding."

"So, what makes you think he was the one who locked you in?"

"I guess because neither of us saw anyone else. If there had been a prowler, surely Trevor would have noticed him running away."

"Not if he was in here guzzling coffee," Brenda said. "Besides, if he did it, why let you out? I mean, what would be the purpose in the first place?"

"To play a bad joke, I guess. It still gives me the willies to pass that door, and that makes me furious all over again."

"Did you ever go back down to see if anything was tampered with?"

Steff shook her head forcefully. "No."

"Did Trevor?"

"I don't know. I didn't ask him."

Still grasping Steff's hand, her friend urged her toward the offices. "Okay. Let's go do it now. He's almost done with your bookcases and we'll never have a better chance."

Steff hung back.

"What's the matter? Don't you want to hear what he has to say?"

"Truthfully, no," Steff admitted. "I've had several opportunities to ask him more about that night and I haven't done it. What if he confesses that he's guilty, after all?"

"What if he really isn't?"

"You have a point there." She sighed again. "Okay. We may as well do it now rather than wait."

Her mind made up, Steff took the lead. They found Trevor putting finishing touches on the new woodwork.

Steff pushed the door open slightly and called to him. "Can we come in?"

"Sure. Just hold your breath."

His voice sounded muffled. Steff knew why when she saw that he was wearing a respirator.

"What do you think?" he asked, stepping back from his work and gesturing with the paintbrush.

"They're beautiful," Steff said. "Look, Brenda."

The other woman agreed. "Very nice."

"Thanks." He dipped his brush into the varnish. "Well, if you ladies will excuse me, I need to finish this coat in one smooth operation so there are no laps."

"We'll go in a second," Steff said. "First, we want to know if you've been back down to the basement."

"Not since the night you had problems with the door," Trevor said cautiously. "I did go look the place over after you left. Why?"

Steff wished she could see his full expression so she could read his emotions more clearly, but the mask covered all but his eyes. "Just wondered. Brenda asked me."

Trevor frowned. "What you really want to know is if I'm the one who locked you in. I already told you I didn't. What more can I say?"

"I wasn't implying that," Steff insisted.

"You were thinking it. I can read you like a book, Princess. I always could." He concentrated on Brenda, instead. "I wasn't going to mention this because I knew it would upset Steff, but I did notice more than just our prints in the dust on those basement stairs. Maybe you can convince her I'm telling the truth. I give up."

"I'll try." Edging toward the doorway, Brenda pulled Steff with her. As soon as they were outside, Trevor shut the door firmly behind them.

"I believe him," Brenda said.

"Why?"

"I don't know. Maybe because of the hurt look in his eyes. I really think he's innocent. Maybe there was somebody else down there, after all."

"Phooey. Those other prints could have been made ages ago and you know it."

"Okay. Maybe the lock malfunctioned when the door closed. Have you thought about that?"

Pausing, Steff stared at her. "No. I hadn't." Although she was still certain someone had pushed her from behind, she glanced at the outer door. "Trevor had left the front wide open that night. I remember because this place was full of moths."

"See? It's possible the whole thing was an accident."

"Possible, but not probable," Steff countered. "Tell you what. Let's try it ourselves."

"Let's not."

The expression on her friend's face made Steff grin. "Don't panic. I'll be the one on the cellar side. All I want you to do is stand by in case it does lock when I slam it. I don't intend to get stuck in there again."

Steff was first to the basement doorway. She stepped through and flipped on the overhead lighting in spite of the faint sunshine coming through the small windows below.

"I'm going to slam the door, then try to open it."

"What if it locks?"

"That's the idea. All you'll have to do is let me out if it does. Ready?"

"No. But I'll help you if you insist. Just be careful."

Steff laughed softly. "Nothing bad can happen to me with you standing right there." Stepping back, she shut the door with a bang. In seconds she'd opened it again. "Well, so much for that theory."

"Thank goodness. Just testing it gives me the shivers."

"Now we need to see if it could have blown closed," Steff said. "Open the front door and check for a breeze."

Brenda did as she was told. "Nope. Not a whisper. How about setting up a fan?"

"Don't bother. Just shove this door closed one more time and we'll quit fiddling with it."

"Okay. You're the boss." She gave the heavy old

door a push. It slammed with a whump and a distinctive click. "Uh-oh."

Steff had heard the same noises. When she tried the handle, the door wouldn't budge. "Twist the knob from your side," she shouted.

"I am. I can't move it!"

"Well, try harder." She heard the lock being jiggled, then footsteps hurrying away. "Brenda? Brenda, where are you going?"

Trying not to panic more than she already was, Steff kept testing the door to no avail. She finally turned with her back to it and stared, wide-eyed, into the murky depths of the cellar.

There was no logical reason to be afraid this time, so why was her heart speeding and her breathing so rapid? After all, it was silly to fear being locked in here. She knew her friend wouldn't actually abandon her.

Steff took a shaky breath and released it with a whoosh. Obviously, Brenda had gone for help. Too bad the only decent set of muscles close by belonged to Trevor Whittaker.

"This is getting ridiculous," Steff mumbled. "That man is going to think I need rescuing every time he turns around."

Unfortunately, that was proving to be more fact

than fiction, as was her tendency for getting into one predicament after another.

Well, it couldn't be helped. And it did prove one important thing. There was a good chance that Trevor had not locked the door when she was downstairs. If nothing else good came of this so-called experiment, at least she felt better about that maddening, enigmatic man.

Staring into the far reaches of the stacks below, she felt unreasonable tendrils of fright start to encroach on her sensibility.

"It's just a room," Steff insisted out loud, hoping that the sound of her own voice would help calm her nerves.

"Yeah," she countered sarcastically, "a dark, scary, forbidding room full of creepy shadows and unseen bogeymen."

Turning to face the door again, she stopped considering her pride and began to shout, "Help! Get me out of here."

SIX

The clomping of Trevor's work boots heralded his approach. He stopped at the basement door and tried the knob. At his elbow, Brenda was wringing her hands and sniffling.

"You didn't do anything but slam it?" he asked her.

"No. Nothing else. Please hurry."

He called to Steff. "You doing okay in there?"

"Just peachy," she answered wryly. "I haven't had this much fun in ages."

"I can't get the lock to work this time," he called through the heavy mahogany door. "I can either oil the mechanism and wait for it to hopefully release or pry it open. Your choice."

"Whatever's faster."

"Okay. Hold on. I'll go get a crowbar from my truck and have you out in a jiffy."

"He's coming right back," he heard Brenda shout as he jogged away. "And don't worry. I'm still here."

Incredulous, Trevor shook his head. If he didn't know better he'd think the princess was getting herself into all these jams to gain his attention. He didn't really believe she'd stoop to such silly tricks, but the idea crossed his mind just the same.

At least this time she'd had a cohort so he couldn't blame the whole situation on Steff. He did wish she'd let him finish his work, though. The sooner he distanced himself from the stuffy collegiate atmosphere—and from her—the better off they'd all be.

He returned with a crook-shaped iron bar and wedged the straight end of it into the doorjamb next to the lock. "Okay. Stand back. This might splinter when it pops loose."

"You want me to go down the stairs?"

"That's the idea. Turn on the lights so you won't be scared."

"They're already on. And who says I'm scared?" Her voice faded as she spoke. "Okay. I'm halfway down the stairs. Go ahead."

He leaned on the bar, felt the door wiggle a little and repositioned his lever to try again. On his third attempt the lock gave.

Steff raced up from the lower level and out into the foyer. At first her eyes were wide and she seemed to be breathing hard, but she quickly composed herself. Brenda, on the other hand, burst into tears.

Trevor stood back and looked askance at them both. "Well, *that* was exciting. Are you ladies through playing games or should I hang on to the crowbar, just in case?"

"We weren't playing," Steff insisted. "However, what just happened does cast doubt on whether you were to blame for locking me in the other night."

"It shouldn't have taken a faulty lock to convince you of that," he replied. "You should have trusted me."

Her lack of a reply or an excuse, however lame, was hard to take. He'd never done anything to lead Steff to believe he was dishonest, yet she seemed unable to trust him. Had she always been that wary? He didn't recall that she had, although ten or fifteen years ago he hadn't been nearly as discerning as he was now.

Then again, if he'd wanted to try to disprove her suspicions he could have gone into more detail about the strange footprints he'd noticed on the dusty stairs the other night. Her insistence that the police not be involved had kept him from following up at the time. There was no way he could have preserved those prints without expert assistance and since Steff was loath to report the incident there was really no way he could hope to prove he'd been telling the truth.

Returning to work, Trevor went through the practiced motions of varnishing the final tier of the shelves while his mind wrestled with the depth of emotion he was beginning to feel for Steff.

Seeing her so frightened had caused him actual physical pain, made him yearn to put his arms around her and assure her that he'd always watch over her, take care of her, so nothing could ever harm her.

That was a ridiculous notion, of course. He was in no position to say anything of the kind, let alone fulfill that kind of promise. Steff was out of his league. Period. And she always would be.

Turning his thoughts Heavenward he murmured a brief prayer for his own sanity, then added, "And, Father, reach out to her and show her how precious she is in Your sight."

Measured against all the things for which he'd prayed in the past, that thought seemed paramount. He'd been selfish to think of Steff on a personal level when he could see he should have been most concerned about her spiritual well-being.

Sighing, he continued to work and pray. "Okay, Father, I think I understand. While You're at it, would You mind giving Steff a good man to love so I can quit daydreaming about her and watching over her to keep her safe?"

Trevor immediately huffed in self-disgust. If he'd thought it was possible to cancel a heartfelt prayer he'd have taken that one back as soon as the words were out of his mouth.

Steff returned to the office she was temporarily sharing with Brenda and flopped into her chair. "Whew! I sure didn't enjoy that experience."

Still sniffling, Brenda blew her nose. "Neither did I. What are we going to do about that broken door?"

"If it were up to me I'd leave it just the way it is," Steff said. "But it's supposed to be locked at night, so I suppose we can't." She took a deep, shaky breath, surprised to find that she was still tremulous.

"How are we going to explain what happened?"

"As briefly as possible," Steff said, beginning to smile slightly in spite of the anxiety she couldn't seem to subdue. "I can imagine what my father would say if we told him we were conducting an experiment that backfired—especially when we were supposed to be working."

"I'd rather not even think about that," Brenda said.

"Yeah. I know what you mean. That's why, before our temporary handyman finishes with my office, I'm going to ask him what he'd charge to fix the door."

"Do you think he will?"

"I don't see why not. He damaged it in the first place, even if it was for my benefit."

"Besides," her friend drawled, "you want him to stick around as long as possible."

"I do not!"

"Liar."

Chuckling, Steff shook her head. "I'm not lying. I may be exaggerating a tiny bit, but I'm telling the basic truth. It has been kind of comforting having Trevor underfoot, particularly when I've needed his help, but it certainly hasn't been relaxing. I'm more confused than ever."

"My mamaw would call that being *bumfuzzled*," Brenda said. "She's a very wise old lady."

"And my grandmother would wash my mouth out if I used that kind of colloquialism."

"Why? It's not a bad word."

"No, but it's not in *Webster's* dictionary, either,

and my family insists upon proper grammar at all times."

"If you don't mind my saying so, your family is so stiff they make those big ole oak trees outside seem positively limber." She giggled. "Sorry. I couldn't resist. You're not going to tattle on me, are you? I really need this job."

"No, I won't tell," Steff assured her. She started for the door. "I'm going to talk to Trevor. Wish me luck."

"How about if I pray for you, instead?"

Sobering, Steff nodded. "Good idea. I can use all the help I can get, especially when it comes to dealing with that man."

She shivered all the way to her bones as she walked away. Trevor wasn't the only reason she needed prayer. She might not be able to put a name to the danger she kept sensing but it was there, just the same. She could feel it every waking moment like a pall that hung over her and the college. And she didn't like that sensation one bit.

Trevor had cleaned his varnishing brush and was picking up his gear when Steff caught up to him.

"I'm almost done here," he said, glancing at her. "You shouldn't put anything on those shelves until next week, if you can help it. I'd like the varnish to cure until then."

"Fine. I'll remember." He could tell from the look on her face that she was pleased with his work even before she looked at him and said, "I'm so glad I asked you to build them. They're beautiful!"

So are you, he thought, although he merely said, "Thanks."

"Before you go, would you mind giving me an estimate on repairing the door we just broke?"

"I do new construction and remodeling, not repair."

"Oh. Well, how about making an exception in this case? I'd really rather not leave the damage until my father or one of the other trustees notices it, and I have no idea who else to call. I suppose I could ask building maintenance to fix it but then there'd be a written report and I'd have to eventually explain what happened."

Trevor could see an unspoken plea in her violet-blue eyes and feel the urging of his heart to give in. "Okay, I'll look at it as soon as I put this stuff in my truck."

"Can I help you carry anything?"

He eyed her warily. "I think not. The last time you helped me we got involved in an argument

over a scrap of trash. I'd rather not do that again,
if you don't mind."

"Which reminds me. Where did you put the
initial we found in the wall? Is it safe?"

He shrugged. "Safe enough, I suppose. Nobody
cares but the two of us, so it's not locked up or
anything. Why?"

"It occurred to me that *I* should be the one to
look after it, especially since it was found in my
office. If you have no objection."

Trevor wasn't happy with her conclusion
because it would just cause him more worry, but
at the moment he couldn't come up with a plau-
sible argument against it.

"None that I can think of," he replied. He
picked up a tote containing his finishing
supplies, then nodded toward the door. "After
you, Princess. Let's go see what your latest
project needs."

"Do you have to sound so disgusted? I mean, I
didn't do it on purpose."

"Didn't you?"

"Of course not!"

He proceeded to his truck, stowed his supplies,
then rejoined her. She was waiting by the splintered basement door and looking perturbed.

"If I do this, it will be strictly as a favor to you," Trevor reminded her.

"And because I'm a Kessler and you want the library expansion contract."

Brows narrowing, he faced her and shook his head. "You really believe that?"

"Of course I do. That's what always happens to me. Just the other night, Dean Rutherford jumped into your Dumpster to help me look through the trash for that initial you'd already taken out. Do you think he'd have done that if Brenda or one of the other staff members had asked him?"

The scowl deepened as Trevor stared at her. "Cornell Rutherford actually climbed into my Dumpster? That's incredible." He paused to consider. "What was he doing here at that time of night?"

"Getting some exercise, I suppose. He wasn't exactly dressed for jogging but he wasn't wearing a suit, either. I was glad to have the company. I've been extra edgy lately."

"I can sure understand that." Eyeing the broken lock and splintered jamb for a few seconds, Trevor turned back to Steff. "Okay. I can do the cosmetic repairs on the frame pretty easily. That old lock is another story. What I'd recommend is replacing the mechanism with one that can be opened from either side."

"Fine, as long as it's done by day after tomorrow. The trustees are meeting then and I'm afraid they'll notice."

"Will they be talking about the library annex?"

"Discussion of it is on their agenda. I plan to show them the wonderful job you've done on my office, too."

"Thanks. If you'd like to see a larger example of my work there's a restaurant in Savannah that we recently finished. It was the first Whittaker job I managed. I'm pretty proud of it."

"What a coincidence! I've been planning to go to Savannah. I promised Lauren and Dee I'd get over their way soon and I haven't yet. It's a perfect opportunity."

"I'd call that more of a God-incidence than a co-incidence," Trevor observed as he unscrewed the lock and pried it from its setting.

"Speaking of convenient things like that, did you have a chance to talk to Mason Grant at the reunion? If you're looking for a list of rich prospective clients, I'd certainly recommend him. He's big in sporting goods."

"So I've heard. Unfortunately, the only thing he

seemed interested in was whether I had an engineering degree."

"You could take extension classes and complete your formal education in the evenings," Steff said. "It would look good on your résumé."

"And then what? Use my diploma to try to impress people like you and your family? No, thanks."

"I didn't mean it that way."

"Oh, come on, Steff. We both know where your priorities lie."

Trevor knew he was speaking too bluntly but he couldn't help himself. The recent time he'd spent being near Steff had left him irritable and stressed. It had also caused him to start to picture her as a permanent part of his life, which was an impossibility. Pressing her to admit their inherent differences was pure self-defense.

She stared at him as if seeing him for the first time. "And you say *I'm* prejudiced? Give me a break, Trevor. My parents may be overly class conscious but I'm not. If I were, I wouldn't be working for a living."

"You just proved my point." He could tell Steff was getting angrier but something inside him kept insisting he had to continue asserting his position, had to make her see how totally unsuited they were for each other.

"What are you talking about?"

"You said it yourself. You don't have to work for a living like the rest of us. How do you think that makes us feel? Huh?"

"Don't be ridiculous. I wasn't trying to lord it over you or anyone else."

"Maybe you don't mean to, but you do it just the same. You can't help it. It's the way you were raised." As he watched, her expression went from one of astonishment to one of sadness, and he started to regret carrying their heated discussion so far.

"Look, Princess," Trevor said quietly. "I'm not trying to criticize you. I'm simply trying to get you to see the truth. As I said before, we are what the good Lord made us and I'm not about to argue with Him. You shouldn't, either."

She faced him with her chin high, her spine straight, her manner unyielding. "You can think whatever you please about me and my family, Trevor. It won't change my attitude toward other people, not even toward you. I'll drive down to Savannah tomorrow. Give me the address of the place you built and I'll look at it. If I'm as impressed as you think I'll be, I'll recommend that the trustees consider hiring Whittaker Construction to build the library annex."

"You'd still do that?"

"Of course. Magnolia College deserves the best and if Whittaker is better than Fowler Brothers, they should get the job."

He didn't know what to say other than "Thank you."

"She's going to Savannah? Are you sure it's not Charleston or Atlanta?"

"I'm positive. You should be safe enough wherever you are right now."

"I wish I could believe that. I've been jumpy ever since I heard the details of what she found in her office wall."

"There's nothing anyone can do about it now."

"Yes, there is. I want you to get that initial and either destroy it or give it to me."

"No way. I might get caught. Why should I risk my good reputation for you?"

"Because, without my silence you won't have a reputation worth saving and you know it."

"What if I can't lay my hands on it?"

"You'd better find a way."

"Don't push me too hard. I could always decide to expose you, you know."

"Don't be ridiculous. There's no way you can hurt me without taking yourself down, too."

Muttered curses followed before "All right. I'll see what I can do. If and when I get my hands on it, I'll phone you again. And in the meantime, I'll hire someone to follow her wherever she goes, just in case."

"Make sure you give a false name so your interest in her can't be traced. And use cash to pay whoever you hire so no one can ID you from that, either."

"Of course. I'm not a fool."

"That remains to be seen. If I don't hear from you in a week I'll…"

"You'll what? Come back to Magnolia Falls and take care of this mess yourself? I very much doubt that."

"Don't tempt me. You never know."

There was a deep sigh, then capitulation. "All right. You've made your point. Be patient. I'll get the initial for you. Somehow."

SEVEN

Steff left home the next day for her drive south along Route 21 to Savannah. The merciless sun beat through the closed Mercedes windows, making her glad she'd worn a light, sleeveless dress and sandals instead of her usual heels.

Approaching the turnoff for the Magnolia Springs State Park on the Savannah River, she shivered in spite of the sizzling outdoor temperature. That park was where Magnolia College had held their end-of-the-term school picnic ten years ago. And that was where and when Adam had died.

Would she ever be able to pass through that area without reliving her poor brother's accident? she wondered. Perhaps. And perhaps it was just as well that she couldn't forget because any memories, even sad ones, kept him alive in her heart.

It had been a beautiful, cloudless day much like

this, she recalled as she pulled to the side of the road and stopped her car on the shoulder. Everyone had been so happy, so carefree. Adam and Penny had recently married, over the Kesslers' vehement objections, and were so in love it was almost painful to watch them together. Adam had doted on his wife and she'd seemed totally enamored with him, too. Of course, at that time, only the two of them had known they were expecting a baby.

"Oh, Adam," Steff whispered. Her hands tightened on the steering wheel. "I wish you could have been there for Penny when she needed you so desperately."

She looked over at the turnoff and began to picture the main landing near the picnic grounds and marina, upriver from the dam. Several of the students in her graduating class had brought pleasure craft and anchored them there for the day. They'd taken turns thrilling passengers and showing off by racing their boats around the lake, leaving sweeping wakes that made smaller boats bob like corks in a tub.

Neither his bride nor the others on the boat at the time could explain how a strong young man like Adam could have fallen overboard and drowned without being noticed. The official police investigation had eventually concluded that his death was accidental.

Poor Penny had been heartbroken in the immediate aftermath of the tragedy and Steff had done all she could to comfort her.

"I can't believe it!" Penny had sobbed. "Where is he? We have to find him." Then she had run to the end of the pier and screamed, "Adam! Adam!" over and over again until some of the other young women had drawn her away from the shore where she had collapsed in hysterics.

Steff had tried to explain everything to her parents when they'd arrived at the lake several hours later. "No one knows how it happened. Adam apparently fell overboard," she had said. "There was a lot of horseplay going on and then he was just gone." Her voice had broken. "They…they found him floating in that inlet over there."

"Your brother was an excellent swimmer," J.T. had countered. "If he wasn't able to save himself there must have been foul play." He had then glared at poor Penny as if she had been personally at fault.

Compassionate and fighting tears of her own, Steff had put her arm around the distraught young woman's shoulders in a show of support. "Penny was on the boat but she didn't see a thing. Nobody did. The men were showing off in the water, that's all. It wasn't her fault, Dad."

"Adam shouldn't have been out here in the first place. He wouldn't have been if it weren't for her. I never did see why he insisted on marrying."

Steff had felt the other woman stiffen beneath her tender touch. Penny had swiped at her tears, then faced the elder Kessler as if he were her worst enemy.

"He married me because we're going to have a baby," Penny announced. She placed her hand flat on her abdomen as she continued. "I'm going to have your first grandchild, Mr. Kessler, whether you like it or not."

That wasn't the way Steff would have broken such startling news but once it was done there was no way to soften the blow. Her mother, Myra, had begun to weep openly and it was all Steff could do to keep from joining her.

J.T. still had plenty to say. "I'll believe it when I see it," he'd shouted. "And until that time, I'll thank you to leave me and my family alone. We want nothing more to do with you."

Remembering that horrible confrontation left Steff's mouth dry and her stomach upset. She remained parked on the shoulder of the road for a few minutes, unable to continue driving when she was overwrought.

It was easy to recall her unsuccessful attempts to smooth things over at Adam's funeral. Penny had acted as if she were alone in her grief and blind to everything around her, including her late husband's relatives. Steff's remaining brother, Luke, had gotten drunk the day before and had stayed that way for a week, her mother had been inconsolable, and her father had acted mad at the world, which was a normal state for him.

All in all, it had been the worst time in Steff's life. Sitting in that chapel, listening to the preacher droning on and on, she had found it impossible to pray.

There were no words to describe her sorrow, no coherent thoughts to comfort her. Her dear, understanding, wonderful brother Adam was gone. Forever. It wasn't Penny or the others on the boat she blamed for his death. It was God.

And did she still blame Him? she wondered. For the first time in a long, long time, she realized she wasn't quite sure.

Glancing in her rearview mirror, she pulled out to reenter the highway. In the distance, parked about a quarter of a mile behind her, she noticed a blue compact car also leaving the edge of the road and merging with the traffic flow.

Had that car been there all the time she'd been parked? she wondered. Maybe. Maybe not. It didn't matter. This was a busy thoroughfare. Surely many vehicles stopped for various reasons all day long.

Still, she kept her eye on the other car as long as she could and was relieved to see it turn off just before she reached the city.

"I'm getting paranoid, jumping at shadows and seeing bad guys in every situation," Steff told herself with a self-deprecating chuckle. And little wonder. If nobody was actually out to get her or to scare her witless, she'd certainly been the beneficiary of an awful lot of odd coincidences lately.

Steff had regained her usual upbeat mood by the time she cruised into central Savannah and passed the elegant bronze statue of the city's founder, James Oglethorpe. To a person who appreciated preserving antiquity the way she did, the city was a living, breathing museum with the charm of the antebellum South. It had been laid out by Oglethorpe in a grid, most of which remained intact, thanks to local historical preservation groups.

Near the Savannah riverfront, many of the

former cotton warehouses had been converted to restaurants, shops and expensive living quarters, although none equaled the grandeur of the original blocks of mansions left in the old city proper.

Dee was waiting for her at the parking lot near the City Market, in front of an Italian Restaurant called Rigatoni's, as promised.

Steff grabbed her purse and digital camera, then joined her friend and gave her the customary hug of greeting. "I'm so glad you could make it. Is Lauren coming?"

"No. Sorry. She was tied up with a client. But you get me, so you're bound to be entertained."

That made Steff laugh. "I don't doubt that for a minute. How's your job going?"

"Fine. Wonderful. Amazing." Dee chuckled as she led the way toward the nearby restaurant. "I'm in PR. What do you expect me to say?"

"Good point."

"So, what's new with you?"

Steff shrugged and slowly shook her head. "I hardly know where to start. You won't believe the crazy stuff that's been happening to me. I'll tell you all about it while we eat. I promise."

Hanging back, she studied the architecture of the Rigatoni's building, then took several quick shots with her camera. The place blended perfectly with its historical surroundings, yet she knew it was the new construction of which Trevor was so proud.

Dee waited for her. "I meant to ask why you wanted to eat here instead of one of the more famous places like Lady and Her Sons or Elizabeth's on 37th. I've never been to this place before, have you?"

"No," Steff answered. "I wanted to check it out because Whittaker Construction built it. Trevor told me he was very proud of the workmanship and I can certainly see why. It's magnificent. Look at the way it fits into the neighborhood. If I didn't know better I'd think it was as old as the other places."

"Ah, Trevor," Dee said with a knowing grin. "Now I know what you meant by crazy stuff. Tell me more."

"All I'm doing is research on builders for the college." Steff smiled at her companion. "And having lunch with a dear friend."

"That's me," Dee said gaily. "Come on. Let's eat early so we can have afternoon tea at the Kehoe House on Columbia Square while you're here. I love their pastries."

"What would your sister say if she knew you were thinking of eating such rich food?"

"Lauren is welcome to her healthy menus," Dee

answered. "As long as she doesn't try to stuff me full of veggies all the time, I won't complain."

"Well, far be it from me to insist we not celebrate," Steff said. "Personally, I'm more than ready for something fattening and decadent."

"My kind of woman," Dee quipped. "Let's go."

As Steff climbed the brick steps leading to the restaurant's stained-glass entrance doors, she was so engrossed in imagining what a beautiful job Trevor's company could do on the Kessler Library addition she barely noted the blue compact car pulling slowly into the parking lot.

"I know Fowler Brothers is adequate for plain construction but they're not nearly as good at capturing ambience and aesthetics," she told Dee. "Their buildings are as bland compared to this one as white bread is to one of those French pastries you mentioned."

Her friend laughed. "Boy, you do have it bad!"

If Steff hadn't wanted to avoid more teasing she might have used her cell phone to call Trevor right then and there. As it was, she could hardly wait to get back to Magnolia Falls to tell him how much she loved his work.

Just his work, Steff insisted to herself. *The man is maddening and hard to understand and so blind he can't see how accepting I am of everyone, including him, whether they come from a moneyed background like mine or not.*

That was what bothered her the most, she concluded. That, and the fact that she wanted him to like her just as she was, not keep trying to prove she should somehow be different.

His problem was that he was seeing her in the same light as he viewed her parents. Perhaps he always had. Being born a Kessler was an advantage in many ways, yet it had its drawbacks, too.

All the denials in the world were not going to be enough to convince Trevor that her heart and mind were open and free from prejudice, she reasoned. The only thing that might make a difference was letting him see continued acts of fairness, including her sincere efforts to get him the library contract.

But I won't be doing it for that reason, Steff insisted. *I'll be doing it because he really is the best for our needs.*

Thinking that made her smile widen. There was a degree of humorous irony in the situation, wasn't there? It was nice to be able to honestly recommend him when that was exactly what she wanted most to do.

* * *

"I hate to tell you this when I know how your daughter feels," the older man said. "But that Trevor Whittaker isn't trustworthy."

J.T. nodded to his old friend, Nat Fowler. "That's what I was afraid of. You don't have to say any more. I'll see to it you get the contract. We've already approved the architectural drawings and I've looked over your cost estimates. It's just a matter of the formal vote and we'll have a contract ready for you to sign."

"How are the fund-raisers coming along?"

"Fine. Don't worry about getting paid. Stephanie assures me we'll have plenty of money in time to break ground as scheduled. She has a few more events planned but we won't have to wait that long."

"Excellent." Fowler rose and extended his hand to J.T. "I'll look forward to hearing from you. How soon do you expect to call for the final vote?"

"In a week or so. I'd like to see the foundation poured before the semester begins and we're overrun with new students."

"Sounds good to me. What are you going to do if your daughter pitches a fit?"

J.T. laughed. "The same thing I always do, ignore her. She'll get over it. She always does."

"That girl needs a husband to keep her in line," the builder said.

"That's what Myra and I keep telling her but she's too stubborn to listen. I'm glad we only had one like her." He sobered. "Lost the best and brightest."

"I know. Adam was special. Well, I'd better be going. Take care and give my regards to your wife."

Watching him leave, J.T. leaned back in his leather desk chair and closed his eyes. The finest detectives money could buy had failed to find evidence of foul play surrounding Adam's drowning, but he knew better. His gut churned. Someone had murdered his eldest son. Whether he was ever able to prove it or not, he knew it as surely as he knew his own name.

If pure hate could have evened the score and brought Adam's killer to justice, J.T. would have already had the pleasure of seeing the responsible party die a horrible, painful, lingering death.

Trevor was at his headquarters, going over invoices, when Steff burst in and startled him. He hadn't thought she'd ever deign to visit a simple office like his, let alone venture onto the wrong side of the tracks to do it.

He smiled. "Well, well. Hello, Princess. What brings you to this part of town?"

"I had to tell you in person," she said excitedly. "I just got back from Savannah. I *love* the Rigatoni building! It's awesome."

"Thank you." He remembered his manners. "Can I get you a cup of coffee or a bottle of water? I'm afraid I don't have anything fancier."

"No, no. I'm not thirsty. I just wanted to see your face when I told you I'm going to recommend you for the library contract."

"Do you think your father will listen to you?"

"He'll have to. I'll make him look at the pictures I took today, for starters. Your work is clearly superior to the Fowler Brothers'. I'm no expert and I can see the difference in quality. Dad will have to agree."

"I hope you're right." He closed the file folder and circled his desk while glancing at his watch. "How about supper? Are you hungry?"

"Not really. I had an enormous lunch and then Dee insisted we stop for afternoon tea so she could have pastry." Steff touched her stomach. "I may never eat again."

"Oh." He should have known she'd have an excuse.

"I might go with you and just have a soda or iced tea," Steff added.

"You will? I thought…"

"I know, I know," she said, making a face, "you thought I was getting uppity again. When are you going to learn I'm not like that?" She began to grin wider. "Well? Shall we?"

"Sure." Trevor escorted her to the door with his hand lightly on her elbow. "We can take my truck if you don't mind riding in it wearing such a pretty dress. Where would you like to go?"

When she said, "How about Burt's Pizza," she could have knocked him over with a leaf of the wild Kudzu vine that everybody predicted was about to bury the South.

Steff was feeling so good about herself and everything else she was taken aback when Trevor reached under the seat of his pickup truck and handed her the now infamous piece of wallboard she'd asked for.

She was so reluctant to touch it again that her hands trembled. "I thought you said it was in a safe place."

"It was. I got it out and brought it with me so I could give it to you the way you wanted."

"Oh." Studying the scrap, she balanced it gingerly in both open palms. "Funny. It doesn't look nearly as menacing as I remembered. I'm not even sure these dots are blood."

"Do you still want to keep it?"

"I guess so. I can always stash it down in the basement with the other old stuff until I decide what to do with it." She looked at Trevor as he drove. "Did you get that door lock fixed today?"

"Yes. I gave three keys to Brenda and left one on your desk. You can lock or unlock the dead bolt from the outside with the key. I was able to make the old knobs work but I fixed them so they won't accidentally lock and trap you again."

"That's a relief. You did leave us a bill, didn't you?"

"Not this time. I figured I could afford to do that little job on the house."

"Then let me buy your supper tonight," Steff said, never dreaming he'd take offense.

"I can afford to eat out, Princess. Tell me, is that why you picked Burt's? Were you trying to let me off cheap?"

"Of course not. Don't be ridiculous. I chose Burt's because it reminds me of all the good times we used to have when we were younger."

Trevor nodded slowly, thoughtfully. "It seems like a hundred years ago sometimes, doesn't it?"

"Two hundred, at least." She sighed quietly, then smiled. "We did have some great times but I wouldn't want to go back."

"Neither would I. I did a few really dumb things in my youth. Things I'm still trying to live down."

"You weren't bad," Steff told him. "You were just a little wild. I think the funniest instance was when you broke into our dorm in the middle of the night and scared everybody to death. That was the most exciting thing to happen in Sutton Hall all year."

"If you and Alicia had answered your phone when I tried to check on you, I wouldn't have had to see for myself that you were okay."

"The phone service was out."

"Yes, but I didn't know that."

"True." Steff reached over and innocently patted the back of his hand as he drove, then quickly withdrew when he turned to stare at her in apparent surprise. Her fingers tingled but that was nothing compared to the shiver that had skittered up her arm and traced her spine when he'd glanced at her.

Folding her hands demurely in her lap, she said, "Alicia and I did appreciate having a big brother looking after us like that."

She paused to see if he was going to respond. Reminding him of their past association had not been accidental. Seeing Trevor as a surrogate family member had been a comfortable, uncomplicated relationship she wished they could recapture. Anything was better than the tension they were experiencing at present.

Lashes lowered, she surreptitiously studied his profile. The good-looking youth was now a ruggedly handsome, mature man. So far she hadn't been able to look at him in the same nonchalant manner she once had. Nor could she forget the genuine concern she'd sensed when he'd freed her from the locked basement the first time and she'd run straight into his arms.

If she closed her eyes she could still relive the moments she'd spent in his solid embrace and see the stunned look on his face when she'd realized her error and had pushed him away.

To her amazement and chagrin, Steff realized that if she had it all to do over again, she might not step back nearly as abruptly. There were some things that were scary and good at the same time, weren't there? And being hugged by Trevor Whittaker was *definitely* one of them.

As for the *truly* scary stuff, the kinds of things

that gave her nightmares… Without serious thought she glanced in the rearview mirror on her side of the truck and noticed a blue car traveling several lengths behind them.

"Trevor?" she said, peering at the image. "Do you think that little blue car back there is following us?"

"What?" He tilted his head to check his mirrors more closely. "Why would you think that?"

"Because I kept seeing one just like it when I went to Savannah." She huffed. "I suppose I'm being paranoid."

"It's not being paranoid if you were actually tailed." His hands tightened on the wheel. "Hang on. I'm going to make a quick turn to see if he follows us."

Glad she was wearing a seat belt, Steff grabbed up the scrap of wallboard so it wouldn't slide onto the floor and braced herself as he gunned the engine and slued around a corner, tires squealing.

Steff's eyes were wide, her heart pounding. This kind of ridiculous thing couldn't be happening. Not to her. She'd always lived a stable, uneventful life. Now, over the course of mere weeks, everything had changed.

She clutched the supposed clue and tried not to tremble. It was impossible. With everything that had happened lately she was as anxious as if she'd just discovered she'd been wading knee-deep in a Georgia swamp full of hungry alligators. She was sick of feeling so disconcerted, so afraid. What had become of her usual self-assurance and poise? She hadn't felt in full control since she'd first been locked in that disgusting basement.

Trevor zigzagged his truck up and down side streets until there was no other traffic evident, especially not any compact blue cars. He slowed to a more normal pace.

Steff studied the road behind them, then sighed. "Whew! I think we're in the clear. That was interesting driving, mister."

"Anything to keep you safe." Trevor pulled over so he, too, could scan the neighborhood more closely. "Looks like we lost him. Maybe seeing that car was just a coincidence. There must be hundreds like it in Magnolia Falls."

A barely perceptible shiver zinged up her spine and prickled the back of her neck. "I sure hope you're right," Steff said. "Because I'm getting awfully tired of jumping at shadows."

"What made you think you were being followed in the first place?"

She shrugged. "I don't know. Instinct?" Beginning to smile and almost ready to laugh at herself, she added, "I seem to have perfected uncalled-for paranoia. My old psych instructor would be so proud."

EIGHT

To Trevor's disappointment, he and Steff were not able to recapture their youthful ease by visiting the pizzeria the way he had hoped they might.

He looked at her across the red-and-white-checked tablecloth. "You sure you won't have a slice? I ordered the kind you like. No olives."

"I suspected that was why you did that," she said, blushing slightly. "I'm amazed that you'd remember."

"I remember a lot about those days," Trevor said softly. "And about you."

He'd yearned to hold her hand ever since she'd touched his hand while they drove. He reached across the table and laid his hand gently over hers, careful to make sure she could easily pull away if she wanted to.

"We can't go back," Steff said wistfully. "Sometimes I wish we could."

"We could never be as carefree as we were then. Too much has happened. We've matured. Learned."

She grinned. "Aged?"

"That, too," he said, mirroring her smile and noting with relief that she had not withdrawn from his touch. "I like to think we're a lot smarter these days."

"We sure thought we knew it all when we were in college, didn't we?"

That made Trevor chuckle. "We sure did. I may not have stuck around long enough to get my degree, but I was just as opinionated as the rest of you."

Steff giggled. "No!"

"Yes, and you know it." He eyed the remaining food. "Like the way I was always trying to get you to eat more. I hope you've noticed I'm not pushing you tonight."

"I thought it was kind of cute back then," she said, her grin spreading to crinkle the corners of her eyes. "But I was worried that you thought I was too skinny."

"You're perfect," Trevor said, hearing an unusual huskiness in his voice and hoping Steff hadn't noticed.

"You're not so bad yourself, Rebel." She leaned back and broke their physical bond. "But I really should be getting home. I have lots of work to catch up on since I played hooky all day."

Realizing their moment of closeness was over, he stood and dropped a tip on the checked tablecloth, then held her chair for her. "You work too hard, Princess."

"Ah, but I love it," she countered. "I don't know if I'd be nearly as diligent if I were doing something I hated."

"I remember you used to have an interest in fine arts," he said as he escorted her to the door. "What happened to those dreams?"

"I find an outlet in decorating for the reunions and preparing fund-raising brochures, things like that. My artistic expertise hasn't gone to waste, if that's what you're getting at."

Trevor chose to drop the subject rather than chance making her angry again. Steff was so defensive of the college and her place there that he knew she'd be unwilling to even consider the idea she might have chosen her job for all the wrong reasons.

They spoke little as they drove back to his office. Half a block away he spotted flashing red and blue lights. "What the…?"

"Is that by your office?" Steff pointed.

"Looks like it." He parked as close as he could get without blocking the police cars. As he jumped out of the truck he shouted, "Stay here."

"Not on your life." She was jogging beside him before he'd gone ten paces. "What could have happened?"

"I don't know."

Approaching, Trevor was stopped by a uniformed officer. "Sorry. You can't go in there, sir."

"It's my place of business," Trevor said. "I'm Whittaker."

The officer nodded. "Okay. Just give our people a few more minutes to check it out so you don't destroy any evidence and I'll let you through."

Steff was clinging to Trevor's arm. "It looks like somebody smashed the front window to get in."

"Well, if they were after expensive tools they were disappointed," Trevor told her. "I keep most of my good stuff either in my truck or at our warehouse."

As the officers who had been inside the building exited, they were waved over by the first man Trevor had encountered.

"This is the owner," the cop said. "Want him to go over the place with you to see if anything's missing?"

When they answered in the affirmative, Trevor paused to speak to Steff. "You may as well go on home. This could take hours and you said you had work to do."

"I hate to leave. Is there any way I can help?"

"Not that I can think of." He glanced across the street at her parked Mercedes. "Just make sure your car isn't damaged before you leave. It looks okay, but after all this, who knows?"

"Okay." In parting, she gave his arm a squeeze before she let go.

Trevor watched her start for her car, then detour back to his pickup. She returned, carrying her purse and the scrap of wallboard, got into her car and drove away.

A sense of menace had begun to encroach on Trevor's thoughts, his gut feelings. He shook it off. This wasn't the first time vandals or druggies had trashed his place. The neighborhood was rundown and slightly seedy, but his overhead was low and his neighbors never complained if he left a few trucks parked on the street overnight. It was a perfect location for a construction business.

Resigned to the inevitable, Trevor followed the officers into his office and began to look it over. Thankfully, his computer was untouched. Whoever had smashed the front window must have been interrupted before they could steal anything worth hocking.

"Thank You, Lord," he breathed quietly.

For no apparent reason his thoughts immediately flashed to Steff. "And take care of the princess for me, will You?" he added. "She's a very special lady."

In the deep recesses of his mind lurked the emotion responsible for his heartfelt prayer. He refused to give it a name but it was there, nonetheless, taunting him, nibbling away at his convictions that he and Steff were an impossible pairing.

I will not give in, Trevor insisted, clenching his jaw. *What I may want and what's right in this case are not the same thing.*

Turning back to the task at hand he forced himself to concentrate on inventorying his spartan office and possessions. That, alone, was enough to reinforce his conclusions that he and Ms. Kessler were worlds apart. They always would be.

"We almost had the initial," the voice on the phone insisted.

"Almost isn't good enough. What happened?"

"I didn't know he'd given it to the Kessler

woman when I broke into Whittaker's office to look for it. I could have saved myself a lot of grief—and the money I spent having her tailed—if we'd known sooner."

"Where is it now?"

"I assume she took it home. My man said he saw her put it in her car but the cops were everywhere because of the burglary. She'd already outrun him once and he said he was afraid of being noticed if he followed her right then." There was a long pause. "I'll wait till tomorrow and get it from her place after she goes to work."

"Call me as soon as you have it. Understand?"

"I will, I will. It's been this long. A few more hours won't matter."

Cursing was followed by "It had better not," before the receiver was slammed down to break the connection.

"I think Whittakers should be given the library job," Steff said firmly as she addressed her father in his home office the following morning.

He was adamant. "Don't be ridiculous. Fowler Brothers has always been the best." He scowled. "Besides, Trevor Whittaker has a bad reputation."

"From his teenage years," Steff countered. "He's not like that anymore. He's matured and he's very responsible."

"Nevertheless."

Placing her palms on her father's desk, she leaned closer to make her point. "Unless you can give me a better reason than that, I'm going to speak to the board myself on his behalf."

Showing disdain, J.T. leaned back in his chair. "All right. Since you insist. I wasn't going to tell you this but I can see it can't be helped. Trevor Whittaker has a lengthy police record."

"How do you know that?"

"I have my sources. And I suggest you stop using him for even the smallest projects before we're robbed blind."

"I don't believe it."

J.T. shrugged, his attitude one of clear dismissal. "Have it your way, Stephanie. The truth is the truth, whether you like hearing it or not. Now, don't you think it's time you got back to work? I know you weren't in your office at all yesterday."

"That's because I was in Savannah, looking at the latest Whittaker Construction company project so I could report on it for you. It's magnificent. I even brought back pictures. Trevor ran the whole job. I know he's capable."

The older man snorted derisively. "It's *what* he's capable of that concerns me. I will not discuss this further. Go to work, Stephanie, before someone catches you slacking and fires you."

Steff was so angry she could hardly speak. Slacking? Her? There was no one who gave more of themselves to Magnolia College than she did. No one. Not even her prestigious ancestors who had founded the place.

Storming out of her father's office, she slammed the door behind her. She had almost reached the front door of the mansion when her mother intercepted her.

"What was all the shouting about?" Myra asked.

"Hello, Mom. Dad and I were just having a spirited discussion."

The older woman began wringing her hands. "Oh, dear. That's what I was afraid of."

"Don't worry," Steff said. "I didn't say what I really wanted to." She urged her mother toward the front door. "Walk me to my car?"

"I don't understand why you and your father can't get along," Myra said as they left the house together. "He never loses his temper with Luke."

"Maybe he should once in a while. Luke could use a good talking-to." She glanced at an upper story. "Is he still in bed?"

"He's been having some rough times lately," Myra said. "You shouldn't be so critical. Your brother has always had a very sensitive nature."

"Do you think that's why he drinks?" Steff asked. "Because it seems to me he's well on his way to being an alcoholic, if he isn't one already."

"We're thinking of sending him to a sanitarium. I keep telling your father it's not necessary but he's been insistent, especially lately."

"Well, for once Dad and I agree about something," Steff said, pausing by her car to give her mother a parting hug. "It will be for the best, Mom. Don't fight it."

Myra began to weep. "I just feel like such a failure. First Adam runs off and marries without even consulting us, then Luke keeps drinking and you…"

"What about me?"

"You know how we feel about your so-called career, Stephanie. Must you continue to shame us?"

After her disagreement with her father and now this, Steff was ready to scream. Instead she merely kissed her mother's cheek, bid her goodbye and slipped behind the wheel of her car.

She was almost to the Magnolia College campus before tears stopped slipping silently down her cheeks.

Trevor was relaxing at home that evening when he heard his sister yell from the opposite side of the duplex they shared. She had jerked open his door and run into his living room before he could go check on her.

"Trevor!" Alicia shouted. "You have to get over to Steff's right away. She needs you."

He grasped her shoulders to hold her still and try to calm her. "What is it? What's wrong? Is she hurt?"

"I don't think so. It's her condo. Somebody broke in and trashed the place while she was at work."

He sat down to lace up his boots. "All right. Tell me exactly where she lives."

As Alicia was speaking, his mind was racing ahead. He knew the area in question and was certain he could find Steff's place without much difficulty. The question was, why had this happened and what might it have to do with the vandalism at his office? Two such incidents, so close together, almost had to be connected.

"Why did she call you if she wants me to come?" he asked.

"She didn't know your home number, I guess. I told her I couldn't leave because the boys are already asleep, and she asked if I'd send you. You don't mind, do you?"

"Of course not." His nerves were enough on edge that he immediately added, "Lock your doors and windows, sis. I don't know what's going on but I don't like the way strange things keep happening around here."

"You think we're all in danger?"

Trevor didn't want to frighten her needlessly but he also felt responsible for alerting her. "I don't know. You have the twins to think of. Just do as I say, okay?"

"Okay. Be careful, Trevor."

He was already running for his truck, his mind reeling. Steff must have been right! She *was* being stalked.

All he could think of was reaching her and taking her in his arms. And that was exactly what he was going to do, whether she liked it or not.

Steff was waiting for him by the curb when he screeched the truck to a halt in front of her building, jumped out and raced over to her. She stepped into his embrace without hesitation.

"You're shaking like a leaf," Trevor said.

"You would be, too, if you'd seen what they did to my beautiful apartment."

"I'm so sorry. Have you called the police?"

Steff shook her head but kept her cheek against his chest. "Not yet. I remembered how they acted at your office yesterday and I thought I might want to look around myself before they made a worse mess than it already is. Besides, I don't have my cell with me."

"I have a phone in my truck. We can call the police from out here."

"Okay. If we have to. But I still don't like the idea. Dad will have a fit when he hears my place was broken into. He's been trying to convince me to move back home ever since I left and this will give him even more reason to insist he's right."

Trevor smiled and gently slipped his arm around her shoulders to guide her. "This is too serious to ignore, and you know it. Come on. I'll dial and you can give the dispatcher the details."

A few seconds later, as he was reaching for the phone, a troubling thought intruded. "Wait a minute. You called Alicia already. Where were you then?"

Steff gave him a funny look. "Um. In my apartment."

"You went in? Alone? What were you thinking?"

"Now don't get upset. I was already in the door before I realized the place had been ransacked. It was natural to drop everything and grab the closest phone."

Once again he embraced her and held her close, his own heart thudding as if it were about to burst. The realization that she could have been hurt—or worse—tore into him as if he'd been sucker-punched. All he could think about was keeping her safe no matter what and knowing it was going to be an impossibility.

I can't do it but You can, Father, he prayed silently. *Please, please, look after her for me.*

In the deepest reaches of his heart he added, *Because, God help me, I think I love her.*

—

NINE

Steff knew she'd begun acting too dependent upon Trevor but she couldn't help herself. The sight of her usually pristine home torn to shreds had shaken her so badly she could barely think rationally, so she had absolutely no objection to his arm remaining around her shoulders. Truth to tell, she relished it.

They followed the uniformed police officers into the apartment and waited in the marble-floored entry hall as requested.

"Nice place you have here," Trevor said.

"You should have seen it before it was trashed," she replied. "It was lovely."

"And expensive."

"There you go again." She took a step away from him and felt his arm relax to fully release her. "You have a severe case of unfair discrimination, mister."

"Whatever." He shrugged as he watched the police pass in and out of view while they searched.

Steff had had a rough day, an even more trying evening, and she wasn't willing to accept his apparent dismissal.

"I don't appreciate you treating me the way my father does, so cut it out." That got his attention.

His head snapped around and he stared. "*What* did you say?"

"That you're treating me just like my father does," Steff repeated firmly. "He acts as if my ideas are sub-par and my choices are idiotic. When I dare to express an opinion, he dismisses it the way he would if it came from a child."

"I don't do that."

"Not in exactly the same way, no," Steff admitted. "But every time you mention how I spend my money, or don't spend it, you're questioning my intelligence and my discernment. I give to charities and support local causes. And with the exception of big things like my car and a few pieces of furniture that were just slashed to bits and will have to be replaced, I manage to live quite comfortably on the wages the college pays me."

"I never said you didn't." One eyebrow arched. "It does surprise me, though."

"I thought it might."

The return of the officers put an end to their private conversation but Steff was certain she'd made her point because Trevor seemed a lot more subdued than he had been. Good. She might not be able to change her father's opinions of her but she wasn't going to permit anyone else to put her down, especially not Trevor Whittaker. A small, adamant voice inside her insisted that she must make him see that she didn't consider herself above anyone else.

Following the police through the apartment, Steff sighed. The mauve sofa and love seat in the living room had been slashed and their stuffing strewed across the beige carpet. There was dark dust from fingerprint powder all over everything.

In her bedroom, the carnage was nearly as bad. Someone had emptied every dresser and desk drawer onto the floor and had taken all her clothing out of the closet as well as clearing those shelves, too. Even her shoes had been scattered.

The sense of being violated was so strong she sagged against the door jamb. "There's no way I'll be able to tell what may be missing in here until I've sorted through it all and put it away," she said with a shaky voice. "I'm sorry. I can't be of any more help than that."

The officer who had been preparing to make a list put away his pad and pen. "All right. Just keep a detailed record and we'll work from that. Pay special attention to missing jewelry and other valuables. I assume you're insured?"

"I have a homeowner's policy."

He touched the brim of his cap. "Then we'll be going. Let us know when you have the list ready. We'll see ourselves out."

"All right. Thanks."

Steff felt as dizzy as she would have if all the air had been sucked out of the room. She took one deep breath, then another before whispering, "I hardly know where to begin."

"Would you like me to stay awhile?" Trevor asked.

Part of her was still upset with him but a more logical facet of her personality insisted she acquiesce. "Yes. If you don't mind?"

He shook his head and gave her a lopsided smile that reminded her of his younger days. "If I minded, Princess, I wouldn't have offered."

"You're not just trying to be nice?"

"Yes, I am. But not because you're a Kessler or because I think you're rich. Okay?"

"Okay. And I apologize for comparing you to

my father. If he were here right now he'd be berating me for not installing an alarm system."

"It was a low blow to compare me to J.T.," Trevor said, his smile spreading. "You really know how to hurt a guy."

"Speaking of bad attitudes, when I told Dad how much I loved your new building in Savannah, he refused to listen. All he wanted to do was run you down by accusing you of having a police record. I told him you were straight and honest, but he just brushed me off the way he always does. I'm afraid Fowlers may get the library contract after all."

"If they do, they do," Trevor replied. "And if the subject comes up again, you can tell your father I haven't had even a traffic ticket in over ten years."

"I wonder where he got the idea you'd been in trouble?"

"I can guess. He and Nat Fowler are old buddies, aren't they?"

"Yes, but…"

"No buts about it," Trevor said flatly. "I had a set-to with some of Nat's men not long ago at one of my job sites. Those guys got hauled off in cuffs, not me. I wouldn't put it past the old man to turn the story around to his advantage."

"Is there proof I could show my father?"

"Probably, but I won't stoop to begging. If Whittaker Construction isn't in the running for the contract, then so be it."

"What did you think when you saw the blueprints?" Steff asked.

The initial astonishment on Trevor's face quickly hardened into indignation. "What blueprints?"

"The ones for the library addition. They were sent out to everyone who asked for them and I know you were on the list because I checked. You must have received them."

"No. I did not."

Speechless, Steff shook her head and sighed deeply before making up her mind. "Okay. Here's what we'll do. You can follow me to the office right now and I'll give you a set of plans. If you can have your bid ready in two or three days, I'll make sure the trustees at least see it before they vote."

"What about your apartment? This mess?"

"It can wait. I can hardly stand being here anyway," she stated with conviction. "Besides, I still have that piece of wallboard in my car and I want to get it into locked storage at the office before anything happens to it."

The expression on Trevor's face reminded her of those cartoon characters with a flashing light bulb suddenly appearing above their heads. His dark eyes widened then narrowed in a scowl and Steff realized that she might have just hit on the reason for both their break-ins.

"Are you thinking what I'm thinking?" she asked.

"If it's about that initial we found, yes." He began to look around the apartment as if expecting a prowler to pop out of the woodwork any second. "I think you should stay at your parents' tonight. For safety."

"I'm not staying here but I'd rather bunk on the floor in my office than go to their house," Steff quipped, trying to lighten the mood and failing miserably.

"No good. You've had problems at work, too."

"I know. I was just kidding. I suppose I could stay with Kate or Jennifer, or even Alicia."

"Just about any place would be better than this apartment, at least until you get the locks changed and install a burglar alarm." He grinned. "And don't tell me I sound like your father again. It's a sensible suggestion, not a mandate."

"I know. And I appreciate your concern. If there's a vacancy at the Mossy Oak Inn, I think I'll get a room there for a few days. It's close to work and I won't be imposing on any of my friends."

She gazed at the clothing on the floor and atop her stripped mattress. "I wish I could wash my things first, though. The thought of wearing any of them after all this gives me the creeps."

"Then do that. I'll follow you to my place and you can give Alicia whatever you want her to wash for you while we're stashing that wallboard at your office. You know she'll be glad to help. She's probably pacing the floor right now, worrying about you, anyway."

"When you're right, you're right," Steff said, beginning to pluck items from the piles and stuff them into a suitcase. "And I think, when I do talk to the police about my missing or damaged items, I'll also give in and mention the initial. They may want to see it."

"Good idea. As a matter of fact, I think you should turn it over to them ASAP."

"You're not going to tell me again that it was just a bad joke?"

Trevor shook his head as he glanced around at the mayhem. "No. This has gone far beyond any joke, even a bad one."

Thankfully, the Mossy Oak Inn had had accommodations available. It was a five-star establishment and worth every accolade it received in guidebooks, from its stunning Gothic architecture and luxurious suites to its outstanding and varied cuisine.

At any other time Steff would have been delighted to stay there. But by the time she had finished at her office, collected her clean clothing and had returned to the inn, she was too exhausted to do more than just shower, crawl into bed and drop off to sleep.

The following morning she telephoned all the trustees except her father and they accepted her suggestion that the final vote on the library contract be delayed an additional week. She almost wished she could see her dad's face when he found out that the others actually valued her opinion!

While Steff was at work, Alicia notified Cassie who called Kate who contacted Jennifer via Pastor Rogers at Magnolia Christian. By the time Steff was through for the day her friends had made arrangements to meet her at her apartment and have a cleaning party as well as another potluck. This time they had assured her they were taking care of everything. All she had to do was show up and give them directions on how she wanted her condo spruced up.

Steff was glad to have plenty of company, especially since she was still jumpy about reentering the ravaged suite. The one thing she hadn't anticipated, however, was that Trevor might also be invited.

The women arrived together, bringing food, beverages and cleaning supplies. Just as Steff was ushering them all in and preparing to close her front door, she spotted a familiar pickup stopping at the curb.

"Oh, good, there's Trevor," Alicia said brightly. "After he told me what a mess your furniture was, I thought we might need some extra muscle so I suggested he drop by. I hope you don't mind."

Steff had to admit her friend's choice was logical. "Not a bit. I suppose I will have to throw some things away. I could have them reupholstered but I'm afraid I'd always see them the way they are now and I'd never like them again."

"I know I wouldn't," Cassie said. "Ugh. Nasty."

Waiting at the door, Steff was surprised to see Trevor circle his truck and pull a stack of pizza boxes from the passenger side.

Her eyes widened as he approached. "Are we expecting more men?"

"Nope. Just me and your gang," he said with a grin. "But if we're going to work, I figured we'd need some real man food, not just those puny little salads you ladies always eat."

In the background Steff heard the others laughing. "We actually eat real food from time to time, too," she said.

"You certainly will tonight." He carried the boxes through the living room and into the kitchen where Cassie and Alicia had cleared the countertop to accommodate the other offerings as well as his.

He unburdened himself then turned to face Steff. "I figured we could drag the worst of the ruined stuff outside and load it into the back of my truck for disposal, if that's what you want."

"Fine. Let's do that right away. I'd rather nuke the pizza later if it gets cold than have to look at my living room the way it is."

Motioning, Trevor led the way. "Okay, gang, I'll take this end of the sofa and a couple of you grab the other side. Think you can lift it?"

Cassie giggled and winked at Steff. "Is he always this bossy?"

"No. Sometimes he's worse," she replied.

"Well, I teach P.E. and I have to exercise to stay ahead of the kids, so I know I can do my part." Cassie hoisted the end of the sofa before Trevor did. "What're you waiting for, Mister Tough Guy?"

As Steff watched them dispose of the couch and love seat she gathered up her slashed accent pillows and added them to the load. Brushing her palms together, she said, "Okay, that's the lot. Let's go eat."

When Trevor hesitated she paused with him. "You're coming back inside, aren't you?"

"Do you want me to?"

"Of course." She smiled, hoping her sincerity showed. "If you think you can stand being in the midst of a bunch of chattering women, we'd love to have you join us."

"I've been listening to Alicia all my life, so I'm pretty used to it," he gibed. "Besides, I want to ask your friends who they may have told about the initial we found on the wall."

"You're not accusing any of them!"

"No, no. But as you just said, women do tend to talk. They may remember mentioning it to someone who showed undue interest."

"Like I did, you mean?" She made a face at him as they started back toward the condo. "If you'd listened to me in the first place and treated that initial seriously, we might have avoided all this."

Thinking he was going to defend himself or argue with her, she was astonished when he merely said, "You're right, Princess. I should have listened to you. I apologize."

Trevor had been as tactful as possible while questioning Steff's friends and they had taken his queries graciously, making him doubly grateful for the ingrained social refinement for which Southern women were well-known. Generally speaking, Southern belles could deliver a barb so smoothly that only a man who had been raised around them would be able to tell if they were being sweet or sarcastic. Or worse.

He, however, was more than aware of their nuances. That was why when Steff looked at him and drawled, "Bless his heart, you've got to love him," he knew it was time to shut up and leave.

Giving her a lopsided smile, he stood and excused himself. "Okay, ladies. I guess I'll be on my way. Is there any more trash to carry out before I go?"

"We put the last three bags in your truck already," Steff said. "Thank you for everything."

"You're quite welcome." His gaze caught and held hers. "Walk me out?"

"Of course."

Trevor waited until they were alone at the curb

before he glanced back at her condo. "Are you planning on sleeping in there tonight?"

"No way. I booked the room at the inn for a week. I wasn't sure how long it would take to clean everything and I didn't want to have to move back here too soon. I may never feel right about this place again. Every shadow makes me jump and even the telephone ringing gives me the shakes."

"I can understand that." He took her hand. "Whatever you decide, be careful?"

"I will. You, too."

She'd entwined her fingers with his and seemed loath to let go, so he tarried. "Remember, you promised to give that initial we found to the police."

"I didn't exactly promise."

Trevor squeezed her hand. "You've got to stop worrying about what your father will say and start being logical, Steff. This break-in was only the most recent incident."

"I suppose you may be right." She sighed. "Okay. I'll stop by the station tomorrow or the next day, after I've sorted through the last of my belongings and take care of everything. So far, I haven't found a single thing to report missing."

"All the more reason to inform them about the

scrap of wallboard. That has to be what started all the trouble."

His brow knit thoughtfully. "I've been giving this whole mess a lot of thought. I'd like to try to set a trap for whoever has been causing us all this grief and I may use the initial for bait."

"Wait a minute. Do you want me to turn it over to the police or not?"

"I do. I plan to make up a fake to use in place of the real one if we decide we need it. All I ask is that you keep this idea to yourself until I've had a chance to figure out exactly what I'm going to do. And when."

"You're going to set this trap at my office?"

"Yes. Our friend, whoever he is, seems partial to the basement there, so that's where I'll wait for him."

"Do you think that plan will work?"

"It should, especially if I'm right about who's been involved. Even if my suspicions are wrong, the idea's still a good one."

"I don't know." Steff folded her arms and hugged herself in spite of the warm evening temperature. "I think I should be there with you as backup, just in case."

"Absolutely not."

"Why not? I'm every bit as capable as anyone

else. I could hide and snap a picture of whoever showed up so we'd have concrete proof."

"And then what?" Trevor asked, not bothering to hide his displeasure. "I don't want you anywhere near that building when I spring my trap. Whoever it is could be dangerous."

"I doubt that," she argued. "He's had plenty of chances to hurt us and all he's done is destroy property."

"And maybe follow you all the way to Savannah and back. This subject is not open to discussion," Trevor said flatly. "You are *not* going to be there. Period. Is that understood?"

Although Steff nodded before she turned and headed for her apartment, he got the uncomfortable feeling she wasn't nearly as genuinely acquiescent as she was acting. He grimaced. What else was new?

If he'd had his way, he'd have become her shadow until they had some answers to their ongoing puzzles. The trouble was, as long as Steff was convinced that she could handle everything herself, there was no way she'd ever agree to let him.

Trevor's only real concern was that the bad guys might be able to get closer to her than he could.

TEN

Steff was worried about Trevor putting himself in jeopardy, but she was positive he wouldn't try anything for at least another week or so because he was involved in the Vacation Bible School program every evening. Then again, so was she, which meant she wasn't free to do any amateur sleuthing, either.

It had occurred to her that since she knew every nook and cranny of the college *she* should be the one to set and spring the trap, assuming they were right about the reasons for the break-ins and their stalker took the bait.

Her only real problem would be coming up with a fake piece of bait the way Trevor had suggested. He might have access to other scraps of old board, but she didn't.

The way she saw it, the only way she could

catch the perpetrator herself was to employ the real piece of wallboard. As long as she kept it near her, day and night, she figured it would be safe enough. Besides, that would also delay the moment when she had to admit she hadn't been in full control of the situation and keep her father out of her hair for a while longer.

There was a slim pocket in the carrying case for her laptop computer, and that was the hiding place she chose. Everyone was used to seeing her lugging that computer case to and from work so it wouldn't seem out of the ordinary if she continued to take it with her wherever she went.

Satisfied, Steff checked her watch. It was nearly five and she was due at the church before six, so she would need to hurry. She closed her computer files and reached for the case containing her laptop and the precious board, then scooped up her purse and headed for the door.

She smiled and shook her head as she pondered the evening she was about to have. "I must have been crazy to say I'd do this," she mumbled. "But I promised Alicia, so I'll go."

However, by the time she'd driven across campus to the magnificent stone edifice that was Magnolia Christian Church, she was having serious second thoughts. The parking lot full of cars did nothing to change that. Her milieu was a boardroom or a ballroom. Being in church had never felt quite right to her.

She parked off to one side, checked to make sure there were no little blue compacts following her, then sat quietly in her car, contemplating. She sure wished she understood children the way Jennifer or Kate or Alicia did. Trevor had been joking when he'd said he might not survive a class of six-year-olds, but she actually felt that way. All she knew about kids was that they were little and confusing. And usually messy.

Sighing, she finally climbed out of the car, grabbed her purse and computer case and headed for the side door where most of the people were entering. No sense delaying the inevitable. Once Alicia saw how uncomfortable she was, she'd probably excuse her for the remainder of the week. At least Steff hoped so, because she'd much rather be hiding in a dank basement and waiting for a prowler than spending the next five nights trying to fool everyone, including herself, into believing that she belonged in church.

Pastor Rogers greeted Steff warmly as soon as she walked through the door, shaking her hand as if he were meeting the most important person on earth.

"Welcome! We're so glad you could come. Alicia told me to expect you."

Steff couldn't help smiling in return. "Well, here I am. Point me to the kitchen?"

"Of course, of course. But first, wouldn't you like a tour of the Sunday school addition? We're very proud of the way it blends with the original stone architecture."

That did interest her. "If you think we have time, I'd love to see it. As you may have heard, we're planning to build an annex to the Kessler Library. I'm always interested in seeing other projects that carry out the style of the older architecture."

She fell into step beside him as he proceeded down the hallway past his office. "Who was your contractor?"

The pastor's smile faded. "Fowler Brothers did some of the earliest work but Whittaker Construction had to finish the job for us. I hate to say anything derogatory about anyone, but the truth is the truth. I'm afraid we caught our first contractor inflating his costs."

"Fowlers? Wow. I'm glad you spoke up. I've been looking for ways to convince my father that they're not the only choice for our upcoming con-struction project. We've used them before and Dad is so sold on them he's blind to other options."

"If you do hire them again, I'd certainly recom-mend that you check their figures carefully. I'm not saying their business practices are always questionable, I'd just be wary if I were you."

Thoughtful, Steff continued the brief tour of the church as she mulled over what she'd just learned. Her father would never believe anything negative about his buddies at Fowlers unless she could come up with concrete proof. What that proof might be, this many years after their last project for Magnolia College, was the question. Even if she did manage to locate some of their old bills, how would she know whether or not they had been padded?

I could ask Trevor, she told herself, before im-mediately rejecting that idea. No. The source of her information would have to be a neutral party, although she couldn't imagine who else might offer to help.

The first thing she'd need to do, she reasoned, was lay her hands on the file containing those specific old records. All that stuff was piled in boxes in the basement beneath her office.

It looked as though she was going to have to

make at least one more foray into that dark store-room if she hoped to prove to her father that Fowlers truly was a questionable choice. Tomorrow, she'd start looking through the old payment records and she wouldn't give up until she'd found what she needed.

Shivering, she vowed that the first thing she'd do was haul those records out of the basement and into the bright daylight. No more hanging out in dark basements when she didn't absolutely have to.

Trevor was surrounded by yammering young-sters when Pastor Rogers poked his head in the classroom and said, "This is our first-grade class. Hi, Trevor. How's it going?"

He looked up, saw Steff with the pastor and grinned. "I'm not sure. You'd better check on me in ten minutes or so and see if these kids have driven me crazy yet."

That made both the children and Steff laugh. He was glad to see her enjoying herself, especially since she hadn't seemed eager to keep her promise to attend, even for Alicia's sake.

Trevor sent her a special smile. "Well, Princess. How do you like our church?"

"It sure doesn't seem as stuffy tonight as it

was when I used to come here with my parents," she answered.

"We have our moments."

A red-haired little boy was insistently tugging on Trevor's hand. He bent down to see what the child wanted, then began to laugh heartily. "My buddy here wants to know if you're a real princess. I told him you were."

"Then it's too bad I left my tiara at home," she quipped. "Maybe I'll remember to wear it tomorrow night."

"You'll be here again?"

"Yes," Steff said, grinning and looking relaxed and happy. "I wouldn't miss seeing how you handle your class. As a former rebel, I assume you'll do fine, but I'd still like to see it."

"Just keep the cookies coming," Trevor said, glancing at the children. "We all know we won't get great snacks if we don't settle down and behave. Right, guys?"

To his relief the room quieted almost immediately. He grinned back at Steff and pretended to wipe perspiration off his forehead with a broad gesture. "Whew. So far, so good. See you later?"

"Absolutely. You know where to find me."

As she accompanied the pastor out of the room

and continued down the hall to the other rooms, Trevor couldn't help grinning. Inviting her to help in the kitchen had actually been his idea and his sister had gone along with it. Now that he'd seen how Steff had reacted to the lighthearted atmosphere in the church, he was thrilled.

He knew that one good experience wasn't enough to undo all her negative memories of worship, but it was a start. Every journey, even a spiritual one, started with a single first step.

Tonight, Ms. Stephanie Kessler had taken that step and Trevor was elated. Now, if he could only get her to trust him the way she apparently trusted so many other people, he'd be the happiest man on earth.

Alicia and Cassie were waiting in the cavernous church kitchen when Pastor Rogers delivered Steff. She hugged the computer case to her as she looked around in awe. "Wow. This place could serve meals to an army. Why is it so big?"

Alicia stood near the gleaming stainless-steel sinks and food preparation tables. "We have a lot of dinners on the ground."

"But you don't actually rough it like folks used to, do you?"

Cassie giggled. "No. We sit at tables, not on blankets on the ground, but the old expression has survived. Didn't you ever attend things like that with your parents?"

"No," Steff said, sobering. "They socialized during and after the formal services but Mother wasn't willing to sit on folding chairs and eat food prepared by strangers, so we never stayed."

"That's a shame."

"Our gang makes up for it by having potlucks." She concentrated on Alicia. "Did you enjoy joining us the other night?"

"I loved it," Alicia said. "All your friends are different, yet they get along fine. It's like most of the people I've met since I started coming to Magnolia Christian. They come from all walks of life, but they really seem to accept and care about each other."

Cassie echoed her sentiment with an, "Amen."

"It is different from the stiff atmosphere I remember," Steff said. "Of course, this meeting tonight isn't really church, it's more like the old Campus Christian Fellowship used to be."

"I beg your pardon?" Cassie was grinning. "This is how our church always is. Did you expect us to run around with long faces and sing dirges?"

That made Steff laugh. "No. Please don't."

"Okay. Come with me. I'll give you an apron and show you around."

"First, let me stash my purse and computer where they'll be safe."

"They'll be fine wherever you leave them," Cassie said. "After all, this is church."

Steff would have liked to accept her friend's simple assurance but she couldn't. Bad things happened everywhere. God must make mistakes. If He didn't, then why had her dear brother Adam's life been taken from him before he'd had the chance to live half of it?

And what about Adam's widow and her little girl? Would a loving, compassionate God have allowed them to remain estranged from the rest of the Kessler family for ten whole years? It didn't seem logical. Or fair.

Closing her mind and heart against accepting divine omniscience, Steff hid her computer behind her purse in a high cabinet and went to work in silence. There were some things she couldn't forgive or forget, and losing Adam was the primary one. Even if his death hadn't been an accident, as her parents had suspected, a loving God could still have rescued him, have saved him from drowning.

She sighed deeply. Not knowing for sure what

had happened was probably the hardest part. Her parents had spent a small fortune on private detectives and still didn't know any more than what was in the original police report.

How could she ever fully trust the judgment of a God who had allowed that kind of horrible outcome to what had begun as a beautiful spring day?

An hour later Trevor had marched his noisy charges to the fellowship hall in a line that had disintegrated as soon as the children spotted the snacks. When Steff glanced over at him, he'd smiled and shrugged before joining her.

"Sorry about that. I thought I had them convinced to act civilized. From babysitting Alicia's kids, I should have known better."

"It's okay. Once they get their cookies and punch, they'll settle down."

He saw her glance past him. When her eyes widened, he turned to see what had caught her attention.

"Uh-oh," she said, "here comes Cassie's brother, Scott, and he's carrying a camera. I have to go."

"Why?"

"To keep my face out of the newspapers, if possible."

Trevor circled the serving table and slipped an arm lightly around her waist. "Nonsense. You're the prettiest woman here. You shouldn't hide."

If she was surprised at his boldness, she didn't show it. He waved at the reporter. "Hey, Scott! Snap one of us, will you? I want a souvenir."

"Sure." The camera flashed once as the young man joined them. "Cassie made me promise to stop by and take a few shots for the local rag. Is she here?"

"In the kitchen with Alicia," Steff said, finally ducking out from under Trevor's arm. Hands fisted on her hips, she faced him. Her expression reminded him of the disgusted look she'd given him the night she'd gotten accidentally locked in the college basement.

He raised his eyebrows. "What?"

"You knew I didn't want my picture taken, so why did you force the issue?"

"Why not? Aren't we good enough to be seen with you?"

"No, I…"

"Well, what is it then?"

She shook her head and made a silly face. "Never mind. Sometimes I forget I'm all grown up and can think for myself. There's absolutely nothing wrong with my being here working and there's not one person in this church I wouldn't gladly invite into my home. There. Does that satisfy you?"

Trevor allowed his smile to develop slowly, lazily, as he gazed at her with affection. "Well, I don't know. You never invited *me* over until you needed a janitor."

"I did so."

"Only by proxy. It was my sister you called when your place was first trashed. I just happened to be the only one available at the time."

"Point taken," she replied, eyeing him from head to toe. "I will say you dress a lot better around here than you did when you were remodeling my office."

Trevor laughed heartily. "You *did* notice the torn jeans! I was beginning to think you hadn't. I had to dig pretty deep to come up with a pair as worn out as those were."

"You did it on purpose?"

"Of course." He was still chuckling. "I remembered how you used to lecture me about my clothes, so I took extra pains to look as grungy as possible." His shoulders shook. "You should see the look on your face, Princess. It's priceless."

Steff rolled her eyes and shook her head. "I can't believe you're still acting like a rebel. Aren't you ever going to grow up, Trevor?"

"Not if it means I won't be able to drive you crazy," he said, grinning with satisfaction. "After all, I have a reputation to preserve."

"Preserving my reputation was why I was trying to hide from Scott," she countered. "But now that he's already taken my picture, I suppose there's no need to worry about it. If my parents don't like opening the morning paper and seeing an image of their only daughter wearing an apron, well, that's just too bad."

"Now you're getting the idea." Trevor lightly patted her shoulder to show support. "Life is short. Don't take yourself so seriously and you'll enjoy it much more."

He saw the spark leave her gaze. Her expression closed, as if she were suddenly remembering sadness and trying to hide it from him.

Steff was hurting. Deeply. He could see it in her eyes, sense it in her very being, and it caused him actual physical pain to watch her endure it.

When had they become so in tune? he wondered. And when had she begun showing him her true feelings instead of always hiding behind her perfectly poised facade?

When she sensed that I was falling in love with her? Trevor asked himself. Although he had never said it out loud, somehow, either consciously or subconsciously, Steff must know how special she was to him.

His only real fear, at this point, was that he might have inadvertently stepped out of the will of God when he'd allowed himself to care so deeply.

And if that was the case, their troubles were just beginning. Still, as long as she was in danger, however obscure, he was going to be there for her. Even if the strain killed him.

ELEVEN

The time she was spending at the inn and the church didn't bother Steff one bit. The idea of returning to her office or apartment, however, continued to set her nerves on edge, and entering the basement again, for whatever reason, promised to be the worst trial of all.

Consequently she'd decided to enlist her co-worker's aid. "I need to make another quick trip to the files in storage," she began.

Brenda's eyes widened. "You're not serious. Not again?"

"Yes, again. But this time I'd like you to stand by the open door and keep me company. You won't have to go downstairs. I'd like you to be close by, that's all. Just in case."

"In case of *what?*"

Steff chuckled softly. "I don't know. Call it insurance, or blame me for being scared silly, if you want. Both are true. It should only take a minute or two to find what I need and haul it upstairs." She grasped the shorter girl's arm to urge her forward. "Come on. I'll slay the dragons. All you have to do is back me up."

"You promise?"

The young woman's overly dramatic reaction helped Steff find more humor in the situation, which, in turn, lifted her spirits. "Yes. I promise. Besides, Trevor fixed the door so we won't have any more trouble."

"Famous last words." Brenda shivered. "I wish he was still here."

Steff wanted to agree out loud but thought better of it. It was bad enough that her waking moments were filled with visions of that man and her dreams refused to let her escape, either. She hadn't had schoolgirl crushes on movie stars when she was young but apparently her ability to engage in hero worship wasn't as underdeveloped as she'd thought.

"What are we looking for?" Brenda asked, pausing at the head of the stairs.

"The financial records from nine or ten years ago. All the boxes are well marked. They shouldn't be hard to locate."

Flipping up the light switch, Steff handed Brenda one of the new keys. "Hold tight to that door and keep it open so you won't need that."

"Gotcha." She managed a weak smile. "Hurry back?"

Steff laughed again as she descended the narrow staircase. "Boy, will I!"

Several minutes later she started back up at a near run. She was carrying a box. The lid was closed.

"Did you find what you wanted?" Brenda asked.

"This is the right year." As Steff left the cellar with a rush, she plopped the box onto the foyer floor and the top fell off.

Brenda gasped. "No wonder you weren't having trouble carrying it. It's empty!"

"It sure is." Steff pressed her lips into a thin line and stared at what should have held the answers to all her questions. "Everything is gone. Everything. I even checked some of the other boxes to see if there'd been a mistake, but I couldn't find anything left from this year or the next. Whoever was prowling around down there apparently got what he was after."

"Who do you think it was?"

"Personally? Someone who's on the side of Fowler Construction. I can't prove it, of course, but everything points to them." She pulled a face. "I'm really ashamed that I suspected Trevor."

"You should be. So, what do we do now?"

Sighing, Steff shrugged. "Nothing. Unless I can convince my father that one of his cronies is a crook, Whittaker Construction doesn't stand a chance of landing the library contract."

"What a shame."

Steff nodded. "Yes, it is. I'll tell Trevor tonight when I see him at church."

"Tonight? Aha! No wonder you were so enthusiastic about helping at VBS. You may be able to fool some folks but I've worked with you long enough to know how your mind works. Admit it. If Trevor hadn't been involved, you'd never have agreed to help, would you?"

Steff wanted to contradict Brenda but found she couldn't honestly do so. She hadn't realized it at the time she'd been talking to Alicia. Now, however, her motives were clear. Trevor's presence *had* made a difference. A big difference. She was not only thinking of him nearly constantly, she wanted to be near him, to hear his voice, to speak with him even if they were disagreeing.

If Steff's parents were upset about a little thing such as her choice of employment or seeing her apron-clad picture in the newspaper, how much more adamant would they be if they knew she was so strongly attracted to a man like Trevor Whittaker?

The notion made her smile. *Attracted?* That was putting in mildly. Like it or not, she was crazy about the guy, and not simply because she seemed to be in constant need of a bodyguard.

Trevor had given a lot of thought to how he might trap whoever had been causing all the trouble. Some of the earlier incidents didn't seem to fit the pattern that had eventually emerged, but he figured he'd understand it all once he caught the perpetrator. His biggest concern was how to implement his plans without Steff sticking her nose into them and putting herself in unnecessary jeopardy.

Finally he decided he'd appeal to her in private after the closing meeting of VBS. He figured he'd take her out somewhere nice, treat her to an expensive meal, then tell her what he was going to do and hope she accepted it. He caught up to her while she and the others were straightening the church kitchen for the final time.

"Good job, ladies," he said. "All the kids were very impressed." He grinned over at Steff. "And thanks for remembering to wear your tiara tonight. My class is convinced you're royalty now."

She giggled and touched it lightly. "My pleasure. I wasn't sure I could even find the thing after all this time. It's not something I have reason to wear often."

"It looks great with your apron," Trevor teased. "I wish your folks could see you tonight."

"The picture Scott took was bad enough," she countered. "My mother was on the phone the morning the paper came out, berating me for getting caught on camera."

"It was for a good cause." He took her aside to add, "How about letting me treat you to a late supper or a cup of coffee?"

Steff glanced at the others. "Some of us had talked about stopping for a latte on the way home."

"You two go on," Cassie quickly said. "We're almost done. Alicia and I can take care of the rest ourselves."

"Well, if you're sure…"

Trevor reached around to untie Steff's apron strings. "Thanks."

"Hey, I never said I'd go with you."

"You'll go." He was grinning as he balled up the apron and tossed it to his sister. "I have some interesting news to share and I know how curious you are. You won't be able to stand the suspense if you turn me down."

"You're pretty sure of yourself, aren't you?"

Trevor laughed. "When it comes to reading you, Princess, I'm a regular genius."

Although Steff was making a face, he knew he had her.

She removed the tiara as she crossed to a cabinet and retrieved her purse and laptop. "Okay. You win. But this had better be good."

"The supper I'm going to treat you to or the news?" he asked, chuckling as ushered her from the room.

She elbowed him in the ribs, then smirked when he flinched. "The news," she said. "Because what I have to tell you in return is definitely not good."

"The trustees granted the library contract to Fowlers?"

"No. Not yet," Steff said with a shake of her head. "But it looks as if I'm never going to be able to prove to my father what crooks they are."

"The Lord will take care of it," Trevor said seriously.

When she looked up at him and said, "Like He took care of poor Adam?" he knew his recent prayers for understanding of her spiritual struggle had just been answered. Too bad the problem wasn't one he could fix.

Instead of going to the Half Joe for coffee and taking the chance of being joined by Cassie and Alicia, Steff suggested they visit Burt's again.

There was no real privacy in the pizza parlor but the noise level was so high that it was practically impossible for anyone to overhear an entire conversation. It was hard enough for Steff to make out what Trevor was saying.

She scooted her chair closer to his and leaned her elbows on the table to finish what she had begun to explain. "When I went to the cellar and checked the record storage box, it was empty. Totally. Whatever was in it had been removed."

"And you think Fowlers are responsible?"

"Them, or someone who wants to keep their past cheating quiet for them." She clasped her hands under her chin. "Maybe we were wrong about this. Suppose it wasn't the clue from the wall that they were after in the first place?"

"Everything that's happened doesn't fit together neatly. I realized that myself a few days ago. The big question is, was the prowler after one thing in one place and something else in your apartment? Or was it even the same person?"

"Neither explains the damage to your office."

"You're right." Trevor leaned back, thoughtful, his brow furrowing. "I guess our next move should be for me to set up the trap I told you about and see who takes the bait."

"I don't like that idea. Not one bit," Steff said. "First, you could get in trouble for being in the administration building without me, especially if something goes wrong and you can't nab the other guy. Second, if someone was after the records instead, he already stole them. We're stuck unless we can convince him he missed some."

"That shouldn't be hard for you. Just tell your dad you've got proof and you'll dig it out of the basement when you have some free time. Word will get around."

"Okay. Suppose that works. What do we do about the other thing? Have you made a prop to use?" Saying that immediately made her reach under the table and touch her computer case to make sure it was still safe and secure. She breathed a relieved sigh. All was well. The case was leaning against her leg, just as she had left it.

At that moment Steff wondered if she should

reveal her change of plans to Trevor. She decided against it. The less he knew about what she'd done with the real initial the fewer lectures she'd be subjected to.

Yes, she knew it was risky to carry the thing around with her. And, yes, she knew she should have already given it to the police. But she hadn't found a single thing missing from her apartment and since she was still rooming at the Mossy Oak Inn, she didn't see any reason to hurry. Whatever the initial stood for, it had lain undiscovered for years and years. Surely a few more days wouldn't make any difference.

Steff told several key people that she was about to reveal a big secret the following day and that her proof was locked up in the basement beneath her office. She knew word had successfully spread when she began receiving queries about it from people she didn't really know.

Trevor had arrived that afternoon, slipped into the basement and simply stayed put. When Steff was ready to go home she made sure she was the last one to leave for the day, then went downstairs to tell him she was preparing to lock up.

The sunlight was fading due to the lengthening

shadows but there was still enough illumination coming through the small, high windows that she didn't need to turn on the overhead lights.

She paused at the bottom step. "Trevor?"

"Over here." He stood.

Steff nearly jumped out of her skin. Her heart was pounding. She placed a hand at her throat. "Oh, dear. I knew you were here and you still startled me."

"Sorry. I didn't want to show myself until I was sure you were by yourself."

"That's okay. You know how uptight I've been."

"We all have. Is everything ready?"

"Yes. I've passed the word all over campus and the rumors are flying. If our prowler is anywhere around, he should be well aware that he missed something in his first attempt."

"What about the initial? Did you mention that, too?"

"Not exactly. I didn't want to sound too careless or naive. But I did insinuate that what I planned to reveal was hidden down here and was very important."

"Good. That should do it. Now go home, Steff."

She hesitated in spite of her still racing heart. "You're sure that's what you want? I could always hide upstairs in my office."

"No. I told you. I don't want you anywhere near here. I have enough to worry about without wondering if you're safe."

"Okay." Her voice gentled to add, "Be careful?"

"I'll be fine as long as I know you're not in danger."

Nodding, she started to turn, then changed her mind and approached him instead.

Resting her hands on his shoulders she placed a fleeting kiss on his lips before he could object, then whirled and ran up the stairs.

Trevor's face had been shadowed when she'd stolen the kiss so she hadn't been able to see his expression clearly and didn't know if he'd been shocked or pleased or upset. At this point it really didn't matter. The kiss had not been something she'd planned, nor had she taken the time to consider what he might think of her for doing it.

All she'd cared about, then and now, was letting him know how much she cared about his safety and how deeply grateful she was for his involvement.

There would be plenty of time to explain her actions in the future. At least, she hoped there would.

Continuing to shiver in spite of the sultry evening, Steff turned off all the lights in the building, locked up, then headed for her car.

Every shadow seemed menacing and the Spanish moss hung from the oaks like specters of evil, hurrying her steps.

She slid into her car and locked the doors. The remainder of her evening was well planned. She drove to the Mossy Oak Inn, then went straight to her room where she dropped off her purse and laptop, changed to running shoes and grabbed her small, digital camera.

When she descended a few moments later she detoured through the kitchen to exit by way of the service entrance and avoid being noticed.

It was a half mile across campus to her office. In less than ten minutes she'd be in a perfect position to hide in the shadows and watch the outside of that building.

She had to do it. She simply had to. For Trevor. No matter how much being outside alone in the dark terrified her, she owed him that much. And more.

"I just heard it's in the basement under the Administration building."

"Then get it."

"I'm not sure I can. I hear they've changed some of the locks."

"You never were resourceful enough. If you

can't steal the new key without being seen, get rough with whoever has it and take it by force."

"I'll be recognized."

"Not if you wear a mask and gloves."

"In Georgia in July? That will attract more attention than if I was running around dressed as a circus clown!"

This time, the laughter was more normal. "All right. You're supposed to be the smart one, so handle it your way. Just get that initial."

"Maybe I should take some other things, too, so it looks like a regular burglary."

"If you'd thought of that in the first place, you wouldn't have nearly as much to worry about now."

"I'm not a common criminal."

"You may not be common, but you're as big a criminal as I am and don't you ever forget it. Do whatever you need to do. Understand?"

"Unfortunately, I'm afraid I do."

TWELVE

The first unusual noise Trevor heard after Steff left was heavy, slow footsteps on the floor above. They weren't those of a woman in heels, like Steff, they were more muffled, as if made by softer shoes. Men's shoes, he decided, holding his breath to listen.

The steps proceeded toward one of the upstairs offices first, then returned and paused at the door to the basement. The lock clicked open. Trevor ducked out of sight.

Slowly, the prowler descended the staircase. Trevor could see his shadow looming but decided to remain in hiding until he saw what the man did next.

Suddenly glass broke behind him. *The window.* Someone else had just shattered one of the small panes at ground level. Heartbeats hammering a staccato in his ears, Trevor hunkered down, held his breath as best he could and waited to see what other disturbing surprises were in store.

The shadowy figure on the stairs froze, too. Trevor realized he was trapped between the stairway and the window. If he moved a muscle he'd surely reveal his position to one or both of the interlopers. The only thing he was glad about was that he'd been firm with Steff. If she'd been down here with him, he'd have been frantic.

The man on the stairs crouched as if ready to spring. The prowler at the window stuck his arm inside, unlocked the frame, then raised it and wriggled through the opening backward. He dropped to the floor with a thud and a muttered curse before switching on his flashlight.

The beam swung across the room in an arc, like the beacon of a lighthouse, then came to rest on the stacks of old records that Steff had carefully arranged as bait.

Trevor knew the burglar wouldn't discover the switch unless he stopped to check dates on the contents of the boxes. He didn't think that was likely. Besides, he intended to stop the theft before it was completed.

His present concern was who the second man

was and what he might be after. Surely, if Fowlers wanted proof of their crooked dealings they wouldn't send two different men to retrieve it.

His jaw clenched. So did his fists. *Of course.* One of the men must be after the old records and the other was looking for the incriminating evidence he and Steff had discovered in her office wall.

It left him with the choice of which man to tackle. He wasn't enthused about taking them both on at the same time, especially not in the dark.

Father, he prayed silently, barely breathing, *what now? What should I do?*

The man on the stairs crept the rest of the way down and stayed in a crouch. Because of his dark clothing, Trevor temporarily lost sight of him.

Across the room, the flashlight played over the stacks of boxes as its holder worked his way closer to both Trevor and the stairs.

Suddenly there was a bright flash from the direction of the broken window. The man who had been wielding the flashlight yelled and doused the beam.

Trevor was temporarily blinded so he knew the others had to be in a similar state. At least, he hoped they were. Before he could lunge at the spot where he'd last seen the flashlight, there was a crashing, scrambling sound.

Someone shouted an epithet that was as much a grunt as it was a curse. Figuring he'd never have a better chance to gain the upper hand, Trevor yelled, "Everybody freeze!"

Dead silence followed. Nothing moved. Trevor's vision was still useless. Colored spots danced in front of his eyes. Arms extended, he started to feel his way toward the area where he'd heard the scuffle.

Someone hit him dead-center with a body slam and sent him reeling into the stacks of heavy boxes. The shelving he collided with began to wobble, then fell.

He raised his arms to try to protect himself but there was no way to stop the avalanche.

The last thing he glimpsed before the darkness of unconsciousness overcame him was someone in black standing over him holding another heavy box. It was raised like a weapon.

Steff heard the struggle inside begin shortly after she snapped the picture through the window. Her first and only thought was for Trevor's safety. She'd taken one other digital photo outside before the prowler had crawled through the broken window, but she could tell it hadn't been clear enough so she'd decided to chance using the flash for her second shot.

What she hadn't considered in her eagerness to capture an identifiable image was what the flash might do to Trevor. Now, however, she was more than worried about him. She was panic-stricken.

She raced to the front door of the Administration building, found it unlocked and jerked it open. Flipping on lights as she went, she saw the basement door ajar.

Without considering her own safety, she shouted, "Trevor! Are you okay?" as she ran toward the stairs.

A dark clad figure barreled up the stairs and crashed into her, spinning her around and nearly knocking her down.

Take a picture, her mind screamed. She'd been gripping the camera in her left hand. She pointed it in the general direction of the fleeing man and clicked the shutter, hoping she'd captured his image.

She was about to turn back to the stairway when she was grabbed roughly from behind.

A gloved hand covered her nose and mouth, stifling her scream. She thrashed. Kicked. Writhed with unbridled anger, determined to free herself.

The strong, masculine arms held her tight. She

couldn't get a breath. The camera slipped from her grasp and crashed onto the hard floor of the foyer with a splintering sound.

Sparks of light flickered at the periphery of her vision. As she began to black out she had time for only one coherent thought. *God, please help me!*

"Steff!" Trevor called. "Can you hear me? Are you up there? Anybody?"

He wasn't certain whether he'd heard her scream or had merely dreamed it as he regained his senses, but he wasn't going to lie here and wonder. Knowing the princess, she could very easily have been responsible for the camera flash that had blinded everyone. It would have been totally in character for her to have disregarded his warnings and put herself in danger by doing things her way.

He pushed the boxes off his legs and rubbed his aching head as he sat up. This evening had definitely not worked out the way he'd planned. So much for playing detective and setting a successful trap.

Trevor stood slowly, painfully, and started for the stairs. The lights upstairs were blazing. If it had been Steff's cry he'd heard, chances were she'd gotten a good look at their prowler. He only hoped and prayed the man had not seen *her.*

Steff came to her senses while being dragged across the campus lawn. Her captor was having to use both arms to carry her and had released her mouth, apparently assuming she'd fainted and would remain unconscious.

She started to resist, then decided to play dead for a few more minutes to give her head more time to clear.

Tears filled her eyes as she thought of Trevor. What had happened to him? Why hadn't he answered when she'd called to him? Was he hurt? Or worse?

The urge to pray was strong. She didn't resist. *Please, God, don't let anything bad happen to Trevor the way it did to Adam. Please? I love him so!*

The heartfelt truth of that statement caused tears to spill out and stream down her cheeks. Would she ever get the chance to tell Trevor how she felt? She had to. She just had to. Even if he didn't feel the same toward her, she was going to swallow her pride and confess her love the first chance she got.

Steff felt her strength returning, her mind focusing. Escape was the first order of business.

She was through allowing herself to be dragged along like a useless rag doll.

Stiffening, she balled up her fist and punched her attacker in the stomach before he could dodge the blow.

He released her with an audible gasp.

She staggered, stumbled, fell.

The man's strong grip closed around her wrist.

"Let me go!" she screeched. "Let me go!"

In the distance she thought she heard someone calling her name just as she was backhanded across the face. She faltered, stunned. Was that Trevor she'd heard?

Imagining that her beloved was looking for her gave her fresh strength. She let herself go limp so the man would either have to tow her or pick her up and carry her, then screamed, "Tre-vor!" with every bit of breath she could muster.

Hearing him answer, Steff was elated. "Trevor!" she shouted again. "Over here. I'm over here!"

To her relief, the man who'd been holding her captive released his hold and fled into the darkness.

Gasping, she slumped to the ground at the base of an oak and struggled to catch her breath. A circle of light from a nearby lamppost illuminated the sidewalk next to the library.

Trevor ran into view.

He came straight to her and fell to his knees to gather her up in his embrace while he showered her hair and cheeks with kisses.

"Oh, Trevor! I was so worried about you."

His arms continued to press her close. "I knew you had to be the one responsible for that flash. What were you thinking? Why didn't you stay away, like I told you to?"

"I couldn't leave you alone," she said, managing to speak in spite of her highly emotional state. "I—I love you too much."

He went very still for a moment, then held her away so he could look into her eyes. "What did you say?"

"I said I love you." She sniffled. "I don't care if you don't love me back. I can't help myself. I *love* you. There, I've said it and I'm glad."

Trevor began to smile and Steff could see more tenderness in his gaze than she'd dreamed possible.

"Is that why you're crying?" he asked.

"No. Of course not." She sniffled again and tried to compose herself. "I'm just happy because my prayers were answered."

He cupped her face in his palms and used his thumbs to wipe away some of her tears of relief as he said softly, "So were mine, Princess. So were mine."

Then he kissed her.

Red and blue lights flashing, two police cars and one unmarked official vehicle converged in the parking lot bordering the Administration building less than four minutes after being summoned. Steff and Trevor greeted the police together and informed them that the attackers had already fled.

"It all started with a break-in, like we told the dispatcher," Steff explained. "We were expecting trouble."

"What about the kidnapping? Who was grabbed?"

"I was. I was trying to take pictures but I dropped my camera and I heard it break when it hit the floor. I'm so sorry. If I'd had the extra memory card in it the way I usually do you might have been able to read that and see if I actually got any pictures of the guy. Maybe you still can. I sure hope so."

She could tell by the scowl on the plainclothes officer's face that she was already in trouble as far as he was concerned. The more details she cited, the deeper his frown grew. Finally she deferred to Trevor and let him finish their explanation while the uniformed officers scoured the building and nearby grounds as directed and also retrieved her camera.

"After both the prowlers ran, I went looking for Steff and caught one of them trying to drag her off," Trevor said in conclusion. He urged her closer to his side and she nestled there gladly.

"Did they get what they were after?" the detective asked.

Steff shook her head. "No. I don't think so. The records I'd left in the basement weren't the right ones and the scrap of wallboard that Trevor and I found earlier is safe in my computer case. I hid it in my room at the inn."

She felt Trevor's grip loosen. He stared. "It's *where?* I thought we'd agreed you'd turn it in to the police."

"I know. I was going to do that just as soon as I was sure we weren't going to need it for bait. I guess the best thing to do now would be to go get it and be rid of it for good, huh?"

She looked to the officer in charge, a middle-aged detective named Jim Anderson whom she knew was acquainted with her father. "If I can have a lift over to the inn, I'll give it to you tonight."

"I think that would be best," Anderson said as he eyed Trevor. "You come, too, Mr. Whittaker."

Steff wasn't at all surprised to hear Trevor say "I don't intend to be left behind." She knew he was angry with her, but she consoled herself with the knowledge that he must return her love, even though he hadn't actually said so.

She cast a sidelong glance at him as they climbed into the backseat of the unmarked car. If she had seen a similar look on her father's face she would have assumed he was irate. Hopefully, Trevor wasn't going to stay mad the way J.T. did, because Steff wanted nothing more than to receive lots of his comforting hugs.

Truth to tell, even when Trevor was so mad at her he looked as though he could spit nails, she still felt safer with him than with anyone else. Being close to him was solace and security, the likes of which she had only imagined in the past.

The only thing she was sorry about was that it had taken a series of crimes to make them finally realize they belonged together.

Steff led the way up to the second floor of the inn. As she reached to insert her key into the lock, Trevor's hand closed over hers.

"I'll do that," he said.

Behind them, Anderson countered, "No. I will."

Steff relinquished the key without argument. How typical of men to insist they had to be the ones to open the door to her suite. Did they think she was a shrinking violet who wasn't brave enough to even unlock her own door?

The idea galled her. So did the uncompromising expressions on both men's faces. The way they were glaring at each other reminded her of two schoolyard bullies going toe-to-toe over some inconsequential thing like being chosen team captain.

The lock clicked. The detective pushed open the door, took one step, then froze and pulled his pistol from its shoulder holster. He studied the scene in front of him for a few seconds before he said, "Stay here. Both of you. I want to check this out before we all go in."

Steff peeked past him. Her lovely room was a shambles! She pressed her fingertips to her lips. It had happened again, just as it had in her condo, only this time the thief may have gotten what he'd come for!

She chanced incurring the detective's further ire by calling to him, "Do you see my laptop case? It's black leather. I slid it under the bed when I left it here."

When he answered, "Just a second," then added

a muffled, "Nope. There's nothing under this bed," Steff knew that her best efforts had been thwarted. If the criminal, whoever he was, had taken her computer case, he also had the piece of wallboard.

Even if the theft hadn't been connected to their earlier troubles and someone had simply wanted to steal an expensive computer, the result was likely to be the same. The authorities would never get a chance to see the bloody initial and no one would ever know who had drawn it, or why.

Discouraged and overwrought, Steff blinked back tears. It was all her fault. Her father was right. She wasn't nearly as smart as she thought she was and now her carelessness had cost the police potentially valuable evidence.

She felt Trevor's closeness, sensed his protectiveness in spite of his earlier manifestations of anger. Looking up at him, she was struck by the kindness and tenderness reflected in his gaze.

"It's okay, Princess," he said softly. "The only thing that really matters is that you're safe."

Steff stepped into his waiting embrace and laid her cheek on his chest. "Do you really think so?"

"Yes." Trevor's voice rumbled in her ear as she slid her arms around his waist and listened to his pounding heart. "Whoever's been causing us all this grief now has what he wanted, one way or another, so we can back off and let the police handle things from here on out."

"I don't know what they can do. Nothing really valuable was taken until tonight. My laptop is the only thing we can prove was stolen, and losing that won't help you get the library construction job."

"There are more important things than getting a contract, Princess. I wouldn't trade you for all the money in the world." He lifted her chin with one finger. "Do you understand what I'm saying?"

Steff had a pretty good idea, but she wanted to hear him speak the words. "I don't know. I can be awfully dense, sometimes. Maybe you'd better spell it out for me so there's no doubt."

That brought a smile to lighten his serious expression. "I love you, Steff. I have for a long time. I was just too stubborn to admit it, even to myself."

"I love you, too," she said through unshed tears of joy. "I don't exactly know how it happened, but I can't imagine my life without you in it."

Trevor gazed at her adoringly. "Are you proposing to me, Princess?"

"That depends. If you're going to drag your feet and waste time trying to talk me out of loving you, then maybe I am."

"Your family will be furious."

"Livid," she said with a spreading grin. "I can hardly wait to tell them."

THIRTEEN

"You got it? Finally?"

"Yes. I overheard the Kessler woman talking to the police outside the library tonight, after she got away from me, so I knew where to look. All I had to do was beat them to it. What do you want me to do now?"

"Destroy it. Wait! What does it look like?"

"It's sort of an initial. The writing's not very clear, so I don't think it's incriminating. I suppose it would be if it really is written in her blood. The splatters sure look like it."

"I don't want to take any chances. Burn it."

"There's plaster inside the scrap. I'll have to peel the paper off to get it to burn."

"Then do it."

"What about the computer? What shall I do with that?"

"Throw it away. Sell it. Pour milk over it and eat it for breakfast, for all I care. Just stop bothering me."

"But what are we going to do about the library annex? When they start it they're liable to find…"

"Nothing. Do nothing. Just keep your distance and see that you don't look guilty if you're questioned later."

"Why would I be questioned?"

There was a harsh laugh before the other person said, "You probably won't be—unless you lead someone to me. If I were you, I definitely wouldn't mention my name. Not if you know what's good for you."

Trevor stayed with Steff until the police had finished examining her room at the inn and taken a detailed report. Since the inn was fully booked, the management had offered to call in a crew of maids to redo Steff's room for that night. She had politely refused. She wasn't up to staying there, especially not after everything that had already occurred.

"I'm ready to move back into my condo," she told Trevor.

"Are you sure?"

Steff nodded. "Yes. The new living room furniture hasn't been delivered yet, but the cleanup is finished, thanks to you and my girlfriends. And I've had the door locks changed. Now I just want to go home."

"I understand. Do you want me to drive you?"

"No, thanks. I'll need my car in the morning. But I would like you to follow me, if you don't mind. I'm still awfully jumpy."

"Little wonder. Have you seen any more sign of that little blue car you thought was stalking you?"

"No. None. It must have been my imagination."

"Good," he said, giving her shoulder a comforting squeeze as he walked her out. When she flinched, he paused to add, "Are you sure you don't want a doctor to check you, first? You might have been hurt when you were being manhandled."

Steff saw his jaw muscles clench and sensed his enormously protective attitude. It was probably a good thing that Trevor had not managed to accost her abductor because both men might have ended up in jail by the time Trevor got through evening the score.

"I'm not really hurt. Just a few sore muscles." She slipped her arms around his waist, stepped into his embrace once again and smiled up at him. "If we were already married you could kiss it and make it better."

"Don't tempt me, woman," he said with a lopsided grin. "You and I have a lot of lost time to make up for."

"I wouldn't dream of arguing with such perfect logic," Steff replied. "All I ask is that you don't tell everybody that I proposed to you instead of the other way around."

"Why not? I thought it was kind of cute."

"You were serious when you agreed, weren't you?"

He held her closer and she laid her cheek on his chest as he said, "Yes, Princess. I was very serious. I want to marry you, the sooner the better. All we have to do is see what dates are open in Pastor Rogers's calendar and reserve the church."

Leaning away slightly to gaze into his eyes, Steff nodded. "I do want to be married in church. I've never thought so before, but since I've gotten to know so many wonderful people who attend Magnolia Christian, I'm sure that's where we should hold the ceremony."

Trevor cupped her face in his hands, his warm palms caressing her cheeks, his voice as tender as his touch. "When you said you thought that God didn't answer your prayers for Adam, I started to see where you were coming from. I wish I could soften that loss for you, Princess, but only God can help you through it."

"I know. He already has. I don't know how it happened but I'm not angry anymore. I'm still sad. I probably always will be. But I'm not blaming God." She managed a smile. "He answered me beautifully when I was praying for your safety."

"He answered you before, too. The answer you got just wasn't the one you wanted."

"I know. Poor Adam. Right now I feel sorriest for my parents, especially Dad. He's not showing any signs of recovering from the loss, and it's been over ten years. Considering the way he feels about spiritual things, he may never get over it."

"I'm so sorry."

Steff's smile grew as she gazed at the face of the man she was going to spend the rest of her life with. "I know you mean that, in spite of the way he's always treated you. Maybe, someday, Dad will see the difference in the way you and I and our Christian friends cope with our troubles and that will soften his heart."

"That's between him and his Heavenly Father," Trevor said wisely. "All you and I can do is pray for him."

"And love each other," Steff added, giving him a quick squeeze before loosening her hold.

To her delight, Trevor said, "Amen," and sealed his agreement with a kiss.

Steff's lips still tingled with the memory of that kiss as she climbed behind the wheel of her car. "I'll drive you across campus to pick up your truck so you can follow me home."

"Fine. I parked behind the library."

She couldn't help giggling as she pulled away from the inn with Trevor in the passenger seat.

"What's so funny?" he asked. "Is it a private joke or are you going to share?"

Blushing, she arched her eyebrows and grinned. "I was just thinking about what I said and it brought to mind what my brothers and I used to say when we wanted a puppy. 'He followed me home, can I keep him?' "

Trevor laughed heartily. "I'm no puppy, but I sure hope you plan on keeping me around."

Steff reached across to touch his hand. "I can't imagine my life without you."

"Did you ever get the dog?" Trevor asked as he turned his hand over to interlace his fingers with hers.

"No. My parents were not the pet-owning type.

I used to feed a stray cat that hung around the gardening shed, but she disappeared soon after my father discovered what I was doing. I suspect he had her carted off to the pound."

"That's a shame. I grew up with pets of all kinds, especially dogs. Maybe I should give you a puppy as a wedding present."

That suggestion made Steff laugh until she considered it more seriously. "How about a little lapdog? One that I can carry around in my purse?"

"Well, that lets out a Great Dane or a Saint Bernard," Trevor joked. "Unless you get a much bigger purse." He sobered. "Actually, I was thinking more of a watchdog, like a shepherd. Something that can protect you."

"That's going to be *your* job," Steff told him. "And judging by the way my life has been going lately, you're going to be a very busy man."

He squeezed her fingers. "My pleasure, Princess."

Two days later Steff arrived at the Kessler estate just after seven in the morning. She was on a mission. A maid admitted her and she found her parents at breakfast. As usual, there was a buffet arranged on the sideboard with enough food for four or five people, which left plenty for Luke, when and if he managed to rouse himself from his latest stupor and join them.

The enormous Duncan Phyfe table was spread with a delicate lace cloth. J.T. sat at the head and Myra at the opposite end. It was she who jumped up and greeted Steff.

"Good morning! Come, sit by me. I'm dying to hear what you've been up to lately." She gestured at the maid. "Another place setting. Quickly."

Steff gave her mother a brief peck on the cheek and chose the chair usually reserved for her brother. "Morning, Mom. This will do fine since Luke isn't here. Just coffee for me, thanks."

J.T. peered around the side of his open newspaper. "We almost never see you unless there's something wrong. What is it this time?"

You mean, besides the fact that I was almost kidnapped a couple of nights ago? She knew her father had to have heard about her close call on campus, yet he didn't bring it up, nor did he commiserate about the rash of burglaries involving both her and the college.

Steff laid a manila envelope next to her empty plate and delayed her answer by pouring cream into the hot coffee she had just been served. She refused to echo her father's gruffness and took a moment in which to compose herself.

Finally she simply pushed the envelope closer to him. "I thought you should see this."

He eyed it as if it were so inconsequential he couldn't be bothered. "What is it?"

"Figures on a recent Fowler Brothers' project at Magnolia Christian Church," she said. "If you'll look closely at the notes I made, you'll see that Fowlers have padded their costs in more than one instance."

Still, he didn't make a move to touch the envelope.

"Go ahead. Open it," Steff urged.

"I don't need to. I've known Nat since he and I were in school together. He'd never cheat me."

"He most likely did cheat you, Dad, whether you're willing to admit it or not."

Her father arched a graying eyebrow as he neatly folded his newspaper and placed it next to his place setting. "And just where did you obtain this supposed proof, Stephanie?"

This was the tricky part. She could lose credibility if didn't choose her words carefully. "I had my suspicions all along. When the records of the last big project Fowlers handled for the college mysteriously disappeared from the basement, I borrowed copies of paperwork from the only other job I had easy access to. The point is, will you look over these figures or not?"

"I may," J.T. said. "Eventually. I'm sure there's a logical explanation for everything, even if it may seem odd on the surface. We've dealt with Fowler Brothers for longer than you've been around and we've always been fully satisfied with their work and their ethics."

"That doesn't mean there haven't been changes in their operations over the years," Steff countered.

Her mother intervened. "Now, now, dear. Your father has always had a wonderful head for business. I'm sure, if there was a problem, he'd have noticed at once."

"Not if he wasn't looking for it." She took another sip of her coffee. It suddenly tasted bitter and she pushed it away. "Well, I'd better be going. Don't get up. I'll see myself out."

Myra's bright orange-and-yellow caftan flowed around her like silk butterfly wings as she followed Steff to the door. "Don't be unreasonable, Stephanie. You know how your father can be when he makes up his mind. There's no sense butting heads with him."

"I'm right, Mother."

"Be that as it may, why do you have to create a conflict every time we see you? Why can't you be more like Luke or…"

"Or Adam? Say it, Mother. You always did favor the boys. Both of you did. I've never been able to do anything as well as they do, or did."

"I never said that."

"No, but you were thinking it. Dad feels the same way. Nobody has to spell it out for me."

"We just don't understand why you insist on having a career, that's all. Your trust fund provides all the income you'll ever need. Why work? We don't see the point."

"I love my job," Steff answered. "Except for Dad's position on the board, I'm the only Kessler who's actively supporting our ancestors' contribution to higher education. You and he should be thrilled, not condemning me for it."

"We don't condemn you, dear," Myra said. "We simply can't see why you must always put yourself first."

"What?"

"You know what I mean. You could be living here with us, or already married and giving us grandchildren, yet you insist on going off and making a career."

This wasn't the first time Steff had heard those opinions expressed and she was tired of trying to overlook them. "You have a grandchild. Adam's daughter."

Myra's lips pressed into a thin line as she shook her head. "No. If she were really Adam's, her mother wouldn't have resisted the DNA testing we asked for."

Sighing, Steff gave up. "All right. Forget I mentioned it. But do try to get Dad to look at those figures I brought, will you? He really should."

"I'll see what I can do," Myra called after her as Steff headed for her car. "'Bye, dear."

Steff's hands gripped the steering wheel until her fingers ached. Once again she had failed in her efforts to be taken seriously. Not only that, she'd had a perfect opportunity to mention her decision to marry Trevor when her mother had brought up the subject and she had let the moment pass.

In retrospect, Steff decided that keeping silent had been for the best. Breaking news like that when her father was already upset would have been beyond foolish. Listening to his rants was going to be hard enough under the best of circumstances.

Right now, what she wanted most was to put her

family and her former life behind her and begin anew. Thanks to the grace of God, she and Trevor had rediscovered their affection for each other.

Judged in comparison to their love and shared faith, everything else seemed inconsequential. Everything else *was* inconsequential.

Trevor was standing outside when Steff arrived at her office. He jogged over and held her car door for her as she climbed out. "Well? What did he say?"

"He didn't believe me," Steff said, shaking her head sadly. "He wouldn't even listen. I don't know why I was surprised but I was."

"That settles it, then." He patted her shoulder for encouragement. "Don't worry. At least we tried."

"There is one more thing we might do," Steff said, looking thoughtful. "Dad went to school with the current Magnolia Falls police chief. If I asked the chief directly, maybe he'd look into the possibility that Fowlers were responsible for helping themselves to the records that disappeared from the basement."

"I hate to see you get more involved. Leave the sleuthing to the cops."

"I will. But it won't hurt to bring it up. Besides,

even if Dad won't believe me, he may believe the chief, assuming some proof surfaces. It's certainly worth one phone call."

Trevor wasn't convinced. "Then I'll do it."

"No. I will. We may as well reap some benefit from the fact that I'm a Kessler."

Trevor slipped one arm around her shoulders as he escorted her to her office. "You won't have to worry about that for long. As soon as you're ready, I'll make you Stephanie Whittaker."

She leaned her head against his shoulder. "Mmm. Sounds wonderful. What did Pastor Rogers say? Is he available?"

"The sanctuary is spoken for until after the first of August," Trevor said, "but he's promised to schedule us soon after that unless you think we should wait and get to know each other better."

"Better than what?" Steff asked. "I've known you for years."

Trevor gifted her with a smile. "Yes, if you count my days of acting the part of a juvenile delinquent. Thinking back, I must have seemed pretty ridiculous."

"Hey, don't worry about it, Rebel. I didn't get the nickname of Princess by being down-to-earth."

That made him chuckle softly and give her

shoulders a quick squeeze before he released her. "You were a pretty stuck-up little thing back then, but I liked you anyway. If you and my sister hadn't been roommates, though, I doubt you'd have given me a second look."

Obviously amused, Steff giggled. "Oh, yeah? I looked plenty, mister, I just didn't want you to realize that I was doing it."

"Well, well. Since it's true confession time, I supposed I should admit that I was as interested in getting to know you as I was in protecting my baby sister. Alicia wasn't the only reason I hung around you two so much."

"It seems we wasted a lot of time, didn't we?"

"Yes, but we can make up for it if we spend the next fifty years or so together."

"That sounds perfect."

He was about to take her in his arms again when Brenda stuck her head through the doorway and grinned at them.

"Morning, folks. What's new? Any more excitement?"

Steff rolled her eyes. "No. It's been several days since Trevor's had to rescue me. I must be slipping."

Her coworker giggled. "Guess so. Listen, if you think you're up to it, your father's on line one. I was just telling him that you weren't in the office yet when you two walked in. Want me to stall?"

"No." Steff circled her desk and reached for the phone. "I'll take it. Thanks."

She sank into her chair and said, "Hello?" as Trevor perched a hip on the edge of the desktop.

"Stephanie. Why didn't you tell me you'd been abducted?" J.T. demanded gruffly.

"I figured you already knew. It happened on campus and you keep close tabs on this place." She paused, unsure whether or not he expected her to elaborate.

To her surprise his voice sounded shaky when he said, "I didn't hear a thing until I talked to Jim Anderson a few minutes ago. I wanted more details on the loss of the records you mentioned this morning and he told me about your kidnapping."

"Everything turned out okay, Dad. Don't worry."

"Worry? Of course I worry. All the time, if you must know."

"About *me?*"

"Yes. Your mother told me what you said about your brothers. I don't know where you got such a ridiculous notion. All my children matter to me. It's just that the boys always seemed to need more guidance than you did and now that Luke is the only son I have left, it's even worse. From the time you were little you were always more capable and levelheaded than your brothers. Maybe that's why they got more attention. It certainly wasn't intentional."

Steff was speechless. Unshed tears misted her vision.

Trevor reached for her free hand as he mouthed, "What's wrong?"

She shook her head. What could she say? What *should* she say? Hearing such a heartfelt confession from her stern, taciturn father was astounding.

J.T. cleared his throat and seemed to have recovered his self-control when he further astounded her by saying, "I not only looked at the papers you brought me, I then discussed the recent rash of burglaries with the police. In detail. They're going to investigate Fowlers for me and let us know if Nat's boys have been up to no good. It certainly looks like they have."

"Thank you," she replied.

"I also heard how Whittaker has been looking after you," her father said. "Tell him I owe him."

"I think you should tell him yourself," Steff said. "He's right here."

When Trevor accepted the telephone receiver,

he stared at it for a second as if it were a live rattlesnake, then put it up to his ear and said, "Hello?"

Steff sat back and listened to the man she loved speaking with her father as an equal. She hadn't been able to pray for her dad nearly as fervently as she'd hoped to, yet her unspoken prayers for his and Trevor's association had apparently been answered just the same.

The conversation was brief. Trevor thanked J.T., bid him goodbye and hung up.

Steff was too curious to keep quiet. "Well? What did he tell you? I couldn't believe all he said to me."

"I'm pretty surprised, too." Trevor began to smile, then to grin. "You're not going to believe this. Your father just promised me he'd try to see that I got the contract for the library annex."

She stood and threw her arms around his neck. "Oh, Trevor! That's wonderful!"

"It's more than that," he said, pulling her close for a kiss. "It's mind-boggling. I'd almost think…"

"What?"

He placed his hands on her shoulders and held her away so he could look into her eyes. "Did you tell him about us? Is that why he offered me the contract?"

"No! Not a word. And if I were you, I'd wait

until the trustees have voted and everybody's signed on the dotted line before I mentioned it."

"Why? Do you think I might lose my new, favored status?"

"Yes," she said, laughing. "I certainly do."

FOURTEEN

It was several more weeks before everything was finalized and Trevor could start digging the foundations for the new annex. He parked near the library, climbed out of his pickup and immediately spotted Steff standing next to his waiting backhoe. That figured. She had never been content to leave details to anyone else, not even a seasoned pro like him. He wouldn't have been surprised if she'd insisted on helping him varnish the bookcases he'd built in her office, as well.

Passing beneath clumps of waving Spanish moss that festooned the massive live oaks, he smiled and waved as he approached. "Morning, Princess. How's my favorite girl?"

Her welcoming grin warmed him far more than the Georgia summer. "Good morning, Rebel. I'd better be your *only* girl."

He drew an imaginary X on his chest. "Cross my heart. Hope you haven't had to wait long."

"No. You're right on time."

"Like I always say, we aim to please." Trevor briefly scanned her casual clothing and noted the canvas gloves she wore. "What are you dressed for?"

"Gardening."

That made him chuckle. "Well, well. You're a woman of many talents. I had no idea you were into gardening."

"Why not? Did you think I wouldn't get my hands dirty?"

"Hey, I never said that."

"But you were thinking it."

"Only because you complained that I ruined your manicure when we tore down the office wall. Remember?"

"Of course. That's why I wore gloves this morning." She pointed at the area next to the sidewalk where he was supposed to begin. "Cassie and I've decided to rescue that beautiful azalea bush."

"It's pretty old. I doubt it'll survive transplanting, especially in all this heat."

"I agree. But Cassie says azalea roots are shallow so we decided to try. I had planned to have it dug out by the time you got here but the ground is awfully hard. If you can scoop it up for us and drop it in this wheelbarrow, we'll take care of the rest."

"Okay. You're the boss."

"You'd better believe it," she taunted.

Her melodious laughter echoed as he climbed aboard the backhoe and went to work. The bucket moved smoothly, deliberately, while Steff stood to one side and watched. As soon as he had broken up the thin sidewalk and uprooted the azalea, she maneuvered her wheelbarrow closer and Trevor was easily able to drop the bush into it.

"Perfect!" Steff said. "I'll just go park this in the shade for Cassie. Carry on."

"Yes, ma'am."

Trevor hoped she'd take her time because he needed to focus solely on this job and when Steff was around, concentration was nearly impossible. Who was he kidding? She was pretty much all he thought about, period.

He swung the boom back and took several more cautious bites of earth, deepening the excavation with each pass. If he hadn't been paying such close attention he might have missed feeling a momentary stutter of the equipment. He peered into the depths of the partially dug trench. Worried that he might have hit buried utilities, he climbed down to take a closer look.

Steff had left her shovel leaning against the building so he dug with it instead of returning to his truck for his own tools. The blade connected with something hard. Trevor peered at it. It looked like…

His breath caught. He dropped the shovel and fell to his knees, frantically clawing at the heavy, wet Georgia clay. With trembling fingers he pushed aside enough dirt to be certain his imagination wasn't playing tricks on him.

He reeled back on his haunches, appalled. These weren't water or electric lines he had unearthed, they were bones. Human bones!

Suddenly a shadow fell across the trench. Trevor leaped to his feet, blocked Steff's view with his body and grabbed her arms to control her. "Don't look."

She frowned at his hands as she tried to twist free. "Why not? Let me go, Trevor. You're getting me all muddy."

"No. There's…" He thought about trying to distract her instead of revealing his gruesome find, then realized she'd never accept anything but the truth. "There's a skeleton in the trench," he said hoarsely. "It's a grave."

"It can't be!"

"I'm afraid it can and it is. I'll stay here and watch so no one disturbs things. You go inside and call the police."

Steff whipped off her gloves, threw them aside and reached into the pocket of her walking shorts. "I won't need to go anywhere. I'll use my cell phone."

Trevor's initial aim had been to get her to leave so he could cover the exposed bones. When she chose to stay with him instead, he decided it was probably for the best since he knew he shouldn't disturb the site any more than he inadvertently had.

That brought him to the sobering realization that, no matter what happened from here on out, he was *not* going to be able to complete his excavations on schedule. The authorities wouldn't care how badly his timetable was disrupted or what financial straits that would put him in. All they'd care about was the poor soul in the trench, which was as it should be.

Keeping his body between Steff and the skeleton, Trevor glanced sideways at it. He wasn't acquainted with forensics other than what he'd seen on television and he supposed those details were less than accurate. Still, the top of the skull seemed small and the arm bone he'd partially uncovered was thin, leading him to surmise that the deceased had been a woman or a young man of slight build.

He wiped his hands on his jeans to clean them as best he could before touching Steff again. He'd left his finger marks in damp clay on her upper arms, temporarily branding her. That was fine with him. Too many weird things had happened on this campus lately for him to relax his vigilance one iota, especially where she was concerned.

Trevor promised himself he'd stick with Steff like glue until they were married. And after that, he was going to stay even closer. God had made her his responsibility and no person or thing was going to harm her. Not while he still had breath in his lungs.

He shivered, thinking of the skeleton in the trench. Someone had loved her or him, too. And someone else had disposed of that body as if it were of no consequence. As if no one cared.

Steff wasn't surprised to see the arrival of the squad cars but she was awed when her own father also drove up.

She and Trevor had been asked to stand back, out of the way, while Jim Anderson and the other investigators worked.

J. T. Kessler not only joined them, he immediately hugged Steff.

Unused to the show of affection, Steff remained a bit stiff. As her father stepped away she noted that his eyes were suspiciously moist.

"I'm glad you were here," J.T. told the younger man as he his shook hand. "The call I got said you found a human body. Is that true?"

Trevor nodded. "Yes. There's no doubt."

"How long do you think it was down there?"

"I don't know. Years, probably. I'd seen some earlier drawings indicating that the utilities for the library had been relocated to run underground near here and I was taking it slow because I didn't want to damage them."

J.T. raked his fingers through his graying hair. "Do you think that's when this happened?"

"I don't know. Maybe."

Trevor noticed that Steff was trembling, so he pulled her closer to his side as he continued to explain. "I suppose the police will run tests that will tell them, but as heavy as that soil is, I can't imagine anyone being able to dig a deep grave at all, let alone refill it without being noticed."

Steff slipped one arm around Trevor's waist before speaking. "He's right. I couldn't even manage to pry up a shallow-rooted bush. It looks to me as though the grave was partially under the old cement sidewalk, too. That was put in while I was still a student here, wasn't it?"

Her father nodded. "Yes. I remember being concerned that the project wouldn't be finished in time for your graduation." He frowned in the direction of all the current activity as he added, "That isn't all I remember, either. I hired Fowler Brothers to move those power lines underground and pour a new section of sidewalk over the top after they were done."

Steff stared her father, then turned to Trevor. Her jaw gaped. "You don't think *they* had anything to do with this, do you?" She looked back at J.T. "Do *you?*"

His color was ashen and his expression one of shock and confusion. "I don't know. A few days ago I would have said absolutely not. Today, I'm not so positive."

"It might explain why they were determined to get this job in the first place," Trevor said. "They would still have had to open the trench for the new foundation, but if they knew what they'd find, they could have done it at night and gotten rid of the evidence when no one else was around."

"That is logical," Steff said. "But when they didn't get the job, you'd have thought they'd have tried to delay the digging."

Her father squared his shoulders, his expression hard. "If I find out that Nat knew about this or was in any way behind what happened to you after the break-in, I'll personally see that he and everyone else on his payroll goes to jail."

Reaching out to comfort him by patting his hand, Steff almost refrained when she was struck by how unnatural the action seemed.

In the split second it took her to decide to proceed, J.T. met her halfway and grasped her hand. The new degree of affection he had begun to demonstrate touched her almost beyond words.

"Don't—don't be too hasty," she said softly. "You and Nat have been friends for years. Surely he can't have known what was going on."

"I hope not." He looked from Steff to Trevor. "If you two are okay, I want to go have a talk with the police."

"We're fine," she assured her father.

Waiting until he was out of earshot, she turned her attention to Trevor. "I still can't believe that's my dad. I keep wanting to ask who stole the real J. T. Kessler and left that nice old man in his place."

Trevor chuckled softly and gave her a squeeze. "I wouldn't let him hear you call him *old,* if I were you. But you're right. He has changed, and for the better."

"Boy, is that an understatement." She sobered. "Who do you think was murdered and dumped in that horrible grave?"

"I don't know. There wasn't anything left but bones, as far as I could tell. I'm sure the police will sift everything in and around it for clues."

Steff gasped as her thoughts focused on past events. "Oh, no! Do you suppose the initial we found was a clue to this murder?"

"There's no reason to think it was. I wouldn't lose any sleep over it."

Shivering, Steff knew Trevor was being sensible, but her imagination refused to be placated. Although she said, "I suppose you're right," her mind kept insisting she was missing something. Something crucial. Something potentially deadly.

She eyed the area where she'd broken free after her attempted abduction, then looked back at the team of experts excavating next to the library.

Never again would she feel safe and at home on this campus.

And never again would she take the health and well-being of herself or those she loved for granted.

There was evil here. It might be masked by beautiful gardens and winding paths shaded by oaks festooned with airy cloaks of Spanish moss, but it existed just the same. It lay beneath the surface, lurking like a hungry alligator, ready to strike at the first sign of weakness or carelessness.

Standing in the crook of Trevor's arm and drawing on his strength, Steff was nevertheless bereft. Magnolia College had been like a second home to her. She'd loved and supported it for literally years.

Yet now, in the wake of the grisly discovery and all of her other trials, she was beginning to view the campus as a place to be avoided. Worse, she was seeing its staff as individuals who might not be as trustworthy as she'd always thought they were.

To her, those feelings were akin to losing her best friend with no possible hope of reconciliation. Her unquestioned fondness for Magnolia College was every bit as dead as the poor soul whose mortal remains had just been unearthed.

"They found her! I told you they would."

"Don't panic."

"Why not? They're bound to figure out who she is eventually, and then what?"

"Then, nothing" came the unnervingly calm reply. "You and I are in the clear just like we were back then."

"How can you be so sure?"

"I'm sure, okay. The only thing that worries me now is how poorly you're dealing with this. After all, you didn't kill her."

"No, but…"

"Don't even say it. I don't want to hear any more from you. Got that? You've done quite enough already."

"I didn't mean for Adam to die. I just wanted…"

"Shut up! You're lucky I had the presence of mind to cover for you then." There was a long, thoughtful pause. "You owe me, big time."

"And I paid you back by covering up your mess. You know that and so do I. I just hope they don't find anything in that grave to implicate either of us."

"Like what? We saw to it that there were no clues left behind. If you'd stopped them from digging there in the first place, the way I told you to, we wouldn't even be having this conversation."

"I don't like it. The whole campus is on edge. I feel as though everybody's looking at me. Studying me. Suspecting me."

"The only reason anybody would think you were

involved was if you acted weird. Just carry on as always. Be yourself. You can do that, can't you?"

"I suppose so. What about you? What are you going to do?"

"Nothing. Absolutely nothing."

"Oh, sure, that's easy for you to say. You're not stuck here the way I am. I don't dare leave or do anything the least out of the ordinary."

"Now you're beginning to understand. Finally. See that you don't forget and you'll be fine."

"Fine?" He huffed with evident self-loathing. "The only way I'd be fine is if I could go back in time and not get involved with you in the first place."

FIFTEEN

Steff went about her daily duties in the ensuing weeks as if she were in a fog.

On the one hand, she was elated because she and Trevor had finally admitted their love for each other. On the other hand, a pall of gloom hung over the campus while everyone speculated as to who had been buried in the makeshift grave and when the murder could have occurred. It was enough to keep her jumping at shadows, as was nearly everyone else she encountered.

Her father had done all he could to keep the story away from the national news, but the details had leaked just the same. As a result, her office had been inundated with queries from alumnae and the families of prospective and current students. Steff had done her best to smooth things over but if Magnolia retained half of her prior enrollment in the ensuing semester she'd be surprised.

Because the local police were not very forth-coming, she'd been forced to answer the many queries with empty assurances. Naturally the au-thorities were treating the death as a homicide and they therefore suspected pretty much every-one including staff, townspeople and former students. Steff couldn't blame them. She just wished they'd finish their investigation, release the site and let Trevor get on with building the library addition.

The one good thing about the confusion on campus was that Trevor had had lots of free time and had spent every spare moment of it with her.

"I was telling Dad that I thought we should assign you your own office since you're here so much," Steff told him with a smile. "He thought I was serious. It was pretty funny."

"I'll eventually bring in the office trailer I park on the site of big jobs, but I'd just as soon hang around in *your* office for now, if you don't mind," Trevor said.

His grin was crooked and slightly embarrassed-looking, further endearing him to her. She reached for his hand and slipped her thin fingers between his strong, callused ones. "Suits me fine. I happen to like having you underfoot."

Pausing to glance at the open office door, Steff shivered slightly and tightened her hold on his hand. "I haven't felt safe since you found the... you know."

"I know. I'm sorry, honey. If there was any way I could have spared you seeing that, I would have."

"It isn't just seeing it," Steff said, "it's knowing that something so dreadful happened here in the first place. I'm still having trouble getting my mind around it. Magnolia always seemed like such a safe haven to me. Now I can barely bring myself to come to work every morning."

"Has your dad been able to pry any details out of his buddies at the P.D.?"

Steff shook her head. "No. Not really. They're as closemouthed with him as they have been with the rest of us. I've learned more from reading the newspaper than I have any other way—and most of that's pure speculation."

"Did you remember to tell the authorities about the guy you spotted lurking in the bushes the night of the reunion?"

She pulled a face. "Yes. They treated my report as if it was of no consequence, the same as when

I told them I thought I'd been followed by that blue car. Since I couldn't ID either person and there were no useful images on my smashed camera, the authorities act as if they don't care."

"I care." Trevor gave her fingers an affectionate squeeze. "At least you're sure it was a man you saw by the library."

"That's all I could really tell. There's no way to know if he was poking around because he knew there was a body buried nearby or if he was there for an entirely different reason. I can't imagine what other reason he might have had, though. The whole thing is just too creepy."

"You're right. Forget I brought it up."

Steff huffed with disgust. "We may as well talk about it. Considering all the crazy rumors that are flying around here, it's impossible not to."

"No doubt." Urging her closer, Trevor gently encircled her shoulders. "How about taking a vacation? Not a real one, just an extended break from all this confusion."

"I can't. I'm needed here. There are more fundraisers to plan and stage, and the police have requested access to my confidential alumni files, too." She wished she'd been allowed to provide those files right away but since the law prohibited her sharing them, she had to wait for the promised court order releasing them.

"It sounds like they think the victim may have been a former student."

"That seems to be the popular consensus around town as well as on campus." Steff briefly laid her head on Trevor's shoulder, then leaned back to look at him. "Suppose I knew the person well? Suppose he or she was an old friend?"

"Let's leave the detective work to the police this time, Princess. You and I have stirred things up enough, already."

"Boy, is *that* the truth. I'd just feel better if we had some solid information."

"Me, too. Did your dad tell you that Nat Fowler's sons were responsible for some of our trouble? The old man was planning to retire and had turned his accounts over to the boys. Apparently they decided their profit margin was too low so they padded the bills for the church."

"But why break in and steal the old records from here?"

Trevor shrugged. "I suppose they thought they could discredit me by pretending I'd ransacked the files. It might have worked if you hadn't decided to trust me."

"Well, it sure backfired. Now they look as if they knew about the murder, too. I don't know why the police haven't arrested them."

"Probably because they were both in Europe for the summer when their father's company was working where we found the body."

Steff shook her head slowly, thoughtfully. "That's too bad. I'd rather tie up all the loose ends and get on with our lives."

"If we put everything on hold until we have the final results of the police investigations, we may be old and gray." He cupped her cheeks in his hands to gaze lovingly into her eyes. "I can't see waiting indefinitely. Can you?"

"No." Steff smiled at him. "I've been giving that a lot of thought, too. I want to get married before my parents have time to turn our simple ceremony into the kind of spectacle the Kesslers are famous for."

"Suits me. I found a nice little house for sale just outside town," Trevor said. "If you approve of it, we could move in there right after the wedding while I build you a castle fit for a princess."

She shook her head. "Trevor, I love you dearly but if you try to build me a castle I will never speak to you again. Don't you understand? I don't want an expensive mansion. All I want is a comfortable home with you and a couple dozen children."

"And a puppy?"

"Okay. And a puppy if that's what you really want. You don't even have to keep pretending the dog is for me."

He made a silly face and acted as if her comments had shocked him. "Me? Pretend? Of course not, Princess." His eyes suddenly widened and he faked a gasp. "Wait a second. *How* many children?"

"I wondered when you were going to realize what I'd said," Steff replied, giggling. "You should see the look on your face! It's priceless."

"That's because I'm still not sure whether or not you're serious. I know you like to tease me, but there are limits."

"Okay." She laughed again. "Maybe only a couple of kids. Is that better?"

"Whew!" He pretended to wipe perspiration off his brow. "That's more like it. I guess I will marry you, after all."

She feigned shock, then stood on tiptoe and leaned closer to kiss him before she said, "You'd better believe it, mister. We've already wasted ten years. I'm not about to let you get away this time."

Trevor tightened his embrace and kissed her soundly. "Who's running away? Not me. I've loved you since you were my sister's roommate. I may have been too dense to realize it then, but in retrospect it's crystal clear."

"I'd never have dreamed it, either," Steff answered. "You and I always seemed to be at odds. I guess we just got so used to playing word games and trying to get one up on each other, we overlooked how close we really were." She smiled wistfully. "I hope we never get so used to each other that we stop teasing and having fun."

He chuckled warmly and kissed her again before he said, "As long as you weren't serious about wanting twelve kids, that's fine with me."

Steff's drawn-out, "Well…" made both of them laugh and share another mutual hug.

"Let's start by going to see that house you found. Now. Today. I don't want to spend one more minute on this campus than I absolutely have to."

As Trevor escorted her outside, his hand rested lightly at the small of her back. Steff wouldn't have had it any other way. She knew she couldn't expect him to continue to spend so much time with her, but as long as the murder investigation was keeping him from working on the library annex she was perfectly happy to have his company. She could hardly remember a moment when she hadn't wanted to be near him.

Gazing around at the campus she'd once loved, she was struck by an unidentifiable feeling of dread that made her shiver in spite of the summer heat. Right now, Trevor was beside her and she felt safe. How would she manage to cope once he went back to work?

Stiffening her spine, deepening her resolve, she assured herself that she was strong and brave enough to face anything as long as she knew Trevor—and God—loved her.

The little, white-painted house Trevor had found for them was everything Steff had hoped it would be, including modest, with a fenced yard in the back and a glorious flood of colorful flowers blooming along the front.

She'd loved the property from the moment she'd laid eyes on it and was delighted when he'd told her his offer had been accepted by the sellers.

"I'll put the deed in both our names," Trevor said as they stood on the quaint wooden porch, holding hands and looking into the backyard where a few abandoned toys still lay beneath a rusty swing set. "You can have it changed once we're married, assuming you're not going to keep calling yourself Stephanie Kessler."

"Not on your life," she said, rolling her eyes and grinning. "I've had all the years of being a Kessler that I can stand. Let Luke carry on the family name."

"How's he doing?"

"Mother says he's fine. I suspect she's over-simplifying but at least he's getting the help he needs. That's a start."

"How about J.T.?"

"Dad's hanging in there. He's still upset over the Fowler fiasco, but he and Nat are speaking again."

Steff slipped her arms around his waist and gazed up at him. "This house is a perfect place to raise a family. It's as if I can feel clouds of love all around us."

"That's my love you're feeling, Princess," Trevor insisted. "I care so much it scares me."

"If that's all that ever scares either of us again, that'll be just fine with me."

"I'll always protect you," Trevor vowed. "Always."

"I know. And just in case you ever need protecting, I'll be there for you, too."

"Okay," he drawled, "as long as you leave your camera at home."

Laughing and joyful, Steff reveled in life itself. God had answered her prayers in a way so far beyond her hopes and dreams that she could scarcely believe it.

She sighed. There were some things about her life and her job that she still wasn't thrilled about, but any drawbacks were overshadowed by the prospect of a peaceful, secure future with Trevor.

She wasn't going to fret about the things she couldn't change or the questions she couldn't answer. As Trevor had wisely said, all they had to do was their best. God would take care of the rest.

Thoughts of Adam tried to encroach on her happiness and she put them in their proper place, refusing to brood.

The past was over and couldn't be changed. It was Trevor's and her future that counted now.

She'd never been happier.

The man stepped outside and paused in the shade of an ancient oak to make the call on his prepaid cell phone. He wasn't about to chance leaving a record of it on the college telephone system. He knew better. That kind of call could be traced.

"Things are starting to settle down here," he said as soon as his party answered. "I thought you'd want to know."

"Good. Have you heard any more about the body? Do they have any leads?"

"No. Nothing." His voice had lowered and he'd cupped his free hand around his mouth.

He paused as a pair of students in navy-and-gold track uniforms jogged past on the expansive lawn, but fortunately they ignored him.

He resumed the conversation as soon as he felt the joggers were far enough away to ensure his continued privacy. "The police still have the site cordoned off and all work on the library has stopped. I can't imagine what else they could be looking for. There was nothing identifiable in that grave with her, was there?"

"Of course not. I told you I was careful."

"All right. I won't call you again unless I hear something definite."

"You disposed of that board with the initial the way I told you to?"

"Yes. I reduced it to a pile of ashes and plaster dust, then put the remains in several plastic sacks and dropped them in different Dumpsters around Magnolia Falls. The best forensics in the world couldn't reconstruct anything identifiable from what I had left."

He shuddered at the memory. He had no proof that the splashes or the letter were actually blood, or that their victim had been trying to leave a clue before she'd died, but he knew in his heart that that was exactly what had happened. Handling that board, destroying it, had left him weak, dizzy and gagging. If he hadn't had such a strong sense of self-preservation he knew he'd never have been able to function well enough to actually destroy it.

"Then we're done," his cohort said. "Go back and tend to your work the way you always do. And while you're at it, give my love to Stephanie."

"You don't really mean that, do you?"

"Of course not, you idiot! If I never lay eyes on any of those people at Magnolia again it will be too soon. I hate them all. You included."

"Then we have nothing more to discuss."

He broke the connection, closed the small phone and slipped it into his jacket pocket. There were some aspects of his life of which he was justly proud, but getting involved with that particular person was not one of them.

Snorting in self-disgust, he turned to reenter the stone edifice. If he were able to look into the mind of each person on staff, how many dirty little secrets would he discover?

Chances were, he wasn't the only one hiding plenty, he decided. As long as he kept his mouth shut and didn't accidentally give any indication that he knew whose grave had been discovered or how the victim had been killed, everything would be all right.

If he'd been a man of faith, he might even have paused and prayed for divine deliverance. Since he wasn't, he simply squared his shoulders, took a deep, settling breath and strode boldly back inside as if he were as innocent as a newborn babe.

* * * * *

In February 2008, be sure to read the second book in Steeple Hill Love Inspired Suspense thrilling REUNION REVELATIONS *continuity,* MISSING PERSONS *by Shirlee McCoy.*

Dear Reader,

This book was a challenge beyond any that I have faced in my career as a novelist and I had to keep reminding myself that the Lord wouldn't ask me to do anything beyond my capabilities. It was a good lesson and one that also holds true for you. Thankfully, He didn't ask me to do it alone. I've dedicated this book to the other five participants in this series for a very good reason. I couldn't have done it without the cooperation and expertise of Shirlee McCoy, Margaret Daley, Carol Steward, Lenora Worth and Marta Perry.

If you feel overwhelmed, look around you. Help is close by. And if you don't have the assurance that you're God's child, I urge you to surrender and ask Jesus to accept you right now. It's that easy.

I love to hear from readers, by e-mail VAL@ValerieHansen.com or at P.O. Box 13, Glencoe, Ar 72539. I'll do my best to answer as soon as I can and www.ValerieHansen.com will take you to my Internet site.

Blessings,

Valerie Hansen

QUESTIONS FOR DISCUSSION

1. Have you ever lived in close-knit community like Magnolia Falls? What about living there was enjoyable? What wasn't?

2. Do you think it's necessary to be highly educated or wealthy in order to be happy? How might it have the opposite effect?

3. Have you ever experienced a creepy sensation and been unable to discover why you felt uneasy? What did you do about it?

4. If, like Steff, you have prayed and not received the answer you expected or hoped for, how did you come to accept it?

5. It's easy to be sorry for things we've done in the past. When have you found it hard to forgive yourself? How did you come to terms with your actions?

6. Like Trevor, have you ever been accused of something you didn't do? Were you determined to set the record straight?

7. Are you part of a church that gives you a strong sense of community and belonging? If not, why not?

8. Is your family cold or distant, like Steff's seems to be, or warm like her relationships with her friends? Who are your greatest supporters?

9. Are you apt to take things into your own hands the way Steff did or are you more easygoing? Do you think she was foolish or simply impatient?

10. Does it drive you crazy, the way it does me, to have to wait to have your questions answered? I like to tie up all the loose ends in my stories—and in my life—but in a series, I don't dare do it or I'd spoil the rest of the books! Are you eager for the next Reunion Revelations story?

LOVE INSPIRED HISTORICAL

*Powerful, engaging stories of romance,
adventure and faith set in the past—when life
was simpler and faith played a major role
in everyday lives.*

*Turn the page for a sneak preview of
THE BRITON
by Catherine Palmer.*

*Love Inspired Historical—
love and faith throughout the ages.
A brand-new line from Steeple Hill Books
launching this February!*

"Welcome to the family, Briton," said one of Olaf's men in a mocking voice. "We look forward to the presence of a woman at our hall."

Bronwen grasped her tunic and yanked it from the Viking's thick fingers. As she stepped away from the table, she heard the drunken laughter of the barbarians behind her. How could her father have betrothed her to the old Viking?

Running down the stone steps toward the heavy oak door that led outside the keep, Bronwen gathered her mantle about her. She ordered the doorman to open it, and he did so reluctantly, pressing her to carry a torch. But Bronwen pushed past him and fled into the darkness.

Dashing down the steep, pebbled hill toward the beach, she felt the frozen ground give way to sand. She threw off her veil and circlet, and kicked away her shoes.

Racing alongside the pounding surf, she felt hot tears of anger and shame well up and stream down her cheeks. With no concern for her safety, Bronwen ran and ran, her long braids streaming behind her, falling loose, drifting like a tattered black flag.

Blinded with weeping, she did not see the dark form that loomed suddenly in her path and stopped dead her headlong sprint. Bronwen shrieked in surprise and fear as iron arms pinned her, and a heavy cloak threatened to suffocate her.

"Release me!" she cried. "Guard! Guard, help me!"

"Hush, my lady." A deep voice emanated from the darkness. "I mean you no harm. What demon drives you to run so madly in the night without fear for your safety?"

"Release me, villain! I am the daughter—"

"I shall hold you until you calm yourself. We had heard there were witches in Amounderness, but I had not thought to meet one so openly."

Still held tight in the man's arms, Bronwen drew back and peered up at the hooded figure. "You! You are the man who spied on our feast. Release me at once, or I shall call the guard upon you."

The man chuckled at this and turned toward his companions, who stood in a group nearby. Bronwen caught hold of the back of his hood and jerked it down to reveal a head of glossy raven curls. But the man's face was shrouded in darkness yet, and as he looked at her, she could not read his expression.

"So you are the blessed bride-to-be." He pulled the hood back over his head. "Your father has paired you with an interesting choice."

Relieved that her captor did not appear to be a highwayman, she sagged from his warm hands onto the wet sand. "Please leave me here alone. I need peace to think. Go on your way."

The tall stranger shrugged off his outer mantle and wrapped it around her shoulders. "Why did your father betroth you thus to the aged Viking?" he asked.

"For one purported to be a spy, you know precious little about Amounderness. But I shall tell you, as it is all common knowledge."

She pulled the cloak tightly about her, reveling in its warmth. "Our land, Amounderness, once was Briton territory. Olaf Lothbrok, my betrothed, came here as a youth when the Viking invasions had nearly subsided. He took the lands directly to the south of Rossall Hall from their Briton lord. Then, of course, the Normans came, and Amounderness was pillaged by William the Conqueror's army."

The man squatted on the sand beside Bronwen. He listened with obvious interest as she continued the familiar tale. "When William took an account of Amounderness in his Domesday Book, he recorded no remaining lords and few people at all. But he did not know the Britons. Slowly, we crept out of hiding and returned to our halls. My father's family reoccupied Rossall Hall. And there we live, as we should, watching over our serfs as they fish and grow their meager crops. Indeed, there is not much here for the greedy Normans to want, if they are the ones for whom you spy."

Unwilling to continue speaking when her heart was so heavy, Bronwen stood and turned toward the sea. The traveler rose beside her and touched her arm. "Olaf Lothbrok's lands—together with your father's—will reunite most of Amounderness. A clever plan. Your sister's future husband holds the rest of the adjoining lands, I understand."

"You've done your work, sir. Your lord will be pleased. Who is he—some land-hungry Scottish baron? Or have you forgotten that King Stephen gave Amounderness to the Scots as a trade for their support in his war with Matilda? I certainly hope your lord is not a Norman. He would be so disappointed to learn he has no legal rights here. Now, if you will excuse me?"

Bronwen turned and began walking back along the beach toward Rossall Hall. She felt better for her run, and somehow her father's plan did not seem so far-fetched anymore. Distant lights twinkled through the fog that was rolling in from the west, and she suddenly realized what a long way she had come.

"My lady," the stranger's voice called out behind her.

Bronwen kept walking, unwilling to face again the one who had seen her in her humiliation. She did not care what he reported to his master.

"My lady, you have a bit of a walk ahead of you." The traveler strode forward to join her. "Perhaps I should accompany you to your destination."

"You leave me no choice, I see."

"I am not one to compromise myself, dear lady. I follow the path God has set before me and none other."

"And just who are you?"

"I am called Jacques."

"French. A Norman, as I had suspected."

The man chuckled. "Not nearly as Norman as you are Briton."

As they approached the fortress, Bronwen could see that the guests had not yet begun to disperse. Perhaps no one had missed her and she could slip quietly into bed beside Gildan.

She turned to go, but he took her arm and studied her face in the moonlight. Then, gently, he drew her into the folds of his hooded cloak. "Perhaps the bride would like the memory of a younger man's embrace to warm her," he whispered.

Astonished, Bronwen attempted to remove his arm from around her waist. But she could not escape his lips as they found her own. The kiss was soft and warm, melting away her resistance like the sun upon the snow. Before she had time to react, he was striding back down the beach.

Bronwen stood stunned for a moment, clutching his woolen mantle about her. Suddenly she cried out, "Wait, Jacques! Your mantle!"

The dark one turned to her. "Keep it for now," he shouted into the wind. "I shall ask for it when we meet again."

* * * * *

Don't miss this deeply moving
Love Inspired Historical story about a medieval
lady who finds strength in God to save her
family legacy—and to open her heart to love.
THE BRITON by Catherine Palmer
available February 2008.

And also look for
HOMESPUN BRIDE by Jillian Hart,
where a Montana woman discovers
that love is the greatest blessing of all.

Love Inspired
SUSPENSE
RIVETING INSPIRATIONAL ROMANCE

Despite warnings to leave Magnolia campus, Lauren Owens couldn't, wouldn't—not when she'd finally found her way back to Seth Chartrand, who'd broken her heart years ago. And not when the cold-case murder remained scarily unsolved—including the young woman's identity. Because Lauren had a sinking feeling she knew exactly who the victim was...

REUNION REVELATIONS

Secrets surface when old friends— and foes—get together.

Look for

Missing Persons
by SHIRLEE McCOY

Available February wherever books are sold.

Steeple Hill®

REQUEST YOUR FREE BOOKS!
2 FREE RIVETING INSPIRATIONAL NOVELS
PLUS 2 FREE MYSTERY GIFTS

Love Inspired®
SUSPENSE

YES! Please send me 2 FREE Love Inspired® Suspense novels and my 2 FREE mystery gifts. After receiving them, if I don't wish to receive any more books, I can return the shipping statement marked "cancel." If I don't cancel, I will receive 4 brand-new novels every month and be billed just $3.99 per book in the U.S. or $4.74 per book in Canada, plus 25¢ shipping and handling per book and applicable taxes, if any*. That's a savings of 20% off the cover price! I understand that accepting the 2 free books and gifts places me under no obligation to buy anything. I can always return a shipment and cancel at any time. Even if I never buy another book from Steeple Hill, the two free books and gifts are mine to keep forever.

123 IDN EL5H   323 IDN ELQH

Name	(PLEASE PRINT)	
Address		Apt. #
City	State/Prov.	Zip/Postal Code

Signature (if under 18, a parent or guardian must sign)

Order online at www.LoveInspiredSuspense.com

Or mail to Steeple Hill Reader Service™:

IN U.S.A.: P.O. Box 1867, Buffalo, NY 14240-1867
IN CANADA: P.O. Box 609, Fort Erie, Ontario L2A 5X3

Not valid to current Love Inspired Suspense subscribers.

Want to try two free books from another series?
Call 1-800-873-8635 or visit www.morefreebooks.com

* Terms and prices subject to change without notice. NY residents add applicable sales tax. Canadian residents will be charged applicable provincial taxes and GST. This offer is limited to one order per household. All orders subject to approval. Credit or debit balances in a customer's account(s) may be offset by any other outstanding balance owed by or to the customer. Please allow 4 to 6 weeks for delivery.

Your Privacy: Steeple Hill is committed to protecting your privacy. Our Privacy Policy is available online at www.eHarlequin.com or upon request from the Reader Service. From time to time we make our lists of customers available to reputable firms who may have a product or service of interest to you. If you would prefer we not share your name and address, please check here. ☐

LISUS07

Love Inspired® SUSPENSE

TITLES AVAILABLE NEXT MONTH

Don't miss these four stories in February

VENDETTA by Roxanne Rustand
Snow Canyon Ranch
After what the McAllisters did to his father, Cole Daniels was determined never to forgive or forget. Then Leigh McAllister landed in danger, and Cole had to decide what was stronger—his old grudge or his need to protect his new chance at love.

MISSING PERSONS by Shirlee McCoy
Reunion Revelations
Lauren Owens had her job and her faith on track, and she looked forward to tackling the mystery back at Magnolia College...until the problem turned deadly. She found herself turning to ex-boyfriend Seth Chartrand for support, for safety and love.

BAYOU CORRUPTION by Robin Caroll
All Alyssa LeBlanc wanted was to distance herself from Lagniappe, Louisiana...and from ace reporter Jackson Devereaux. But once she witnessed the attack on the sheriff, she knew she couldn't walk away. Working with Jackson, Alyssa investigated the crime—and uncovered her past.

LETHAL DECEPTION by Lynette Eason
When guerillas held Cassidy McKnight captive in the Amazon, ex-Navy SEAL turned E.R. doctor Gabe Sinclair returned to his military roots to rescue her. He thought the job was done, yet danger followed Cassidy home....

LISCNM0108